War

NAT LOGAN

Playlist

The Boys Are Back In Town, Thin Lizzy
Best of You, Foo Fighters
Go Find Less, Riley Roth
I'll Be There for You, Meghan Trainor
Broken & Beautiful, Kelly Clarkson
Run Like The River, Meghan Trainor
Road Less Traveled, Meghan Trainor
One of Them Girls, Lee Brice
It Ain't My Fault, Brothers Osborne
Soul, Lee Brice
Someone Like You, Adele
Waffle House, Jonas Brothers
One Shot, Hunter Hayes
Rumor, Lee Brice, Bryan Todd
Best of You, Andy Grammer, Elle King
Could Have Been Me, Halsey
Fictional, Khloe Rose
Somewhere Only We Know, Keane
I Wanna Dance with Somebody, Whitney Houston
Honky Tonk Badonkadonk, Trace Adkins

Dedication

To all of you who have found your one, lost your one or still looking for your one- sometimes we find our other half when we weren't looking.

Author's Acknowledgements

My books don't make it to publication without a huge amount of help. Thank you to the bottom of my heart to my editors, Ink It Out Editing and My Notes in the Margin. Taking a book from an idea to a fully written book is a labor of love which includes a lot of ups and downs. Thank you to my PA and alpha reader Beth. Without you talking me off a ledge or out of the hole I'd written myself into, this book wouldn't be published.

Now, if you've read the prequel, you might notice a couple of changes. I didn't have the Bluff Creek Brotherhood MC fully figured out when I wrote the prequel story. If you have any questions after reading the book, come find me in my reader group on FB Steamy Swoony Romance Reads and we can chat.

Now, grab a drink and settle back. Welcome to the Bluff Creek Brotherhood MC and the world of the women of Franks and Daughters Bail Bonds. It's time for a ride.

Codes

Code Monica: Everything's perfect. No injuries.

Code Ross: Everything's not okay. Help needed.

Code Janice: Going radio silent.

Code Rachel: Emotional backup needed. No questions asked.

Code Phoebe: Be ready with backup. Something's off but nothing pinpointed.

Code Chandler: Friendlies incoming.

Code Joey: Targets neutralized. Medical attention may be needed.

Code Burke: The old guys or originals have it.

Code Pancakes: The sisters lost their mom before the new codes were used. Pancakes were Kathryn's code for solving any problem. They'd meet around the table with pancakes and bacon and work through any problems. It stuck.

Chapter One

War jerked awake at the sound of banging on his door. He moved the papers off his lap, kicking the recliner into the upright position. He'd fallen asleep going over the MC's different businesses. At forty-three he didn't feel old but for him to fall asleep in the afternoon said otherwise.

He'd hidden out in his room because Saturdays were crazy. Between everyone getting ready for the weekly party and the originals deciding they needed to liven things up, he'd craved a little quiet. Three months back he still felt like he was treading water. His view of what it took to be the president of the MC and a second-generation legacy had been skewed.

His door shook as the pounding started again.

"War, get out here."

He stood, grabbed his cut from its hanger and slid it on, then grabbed his gun. Bear was his best friend but if he'd woken him up for some stupid shit, he just might shoot him. Grabbing the door, he swung it open.

"What?"

Bear shook his head, looking toward the ceiling, and then pointed toward the front of the clubhouse. War brushed past Bear, heading down the hall. Roam, his twin, waited by the hallway, hiding a smile behind his hand.

He'd wanted this. He'd dreamed of being president of the Bluff Creek Brotherhood MC since he was old enough to understand what it meant. He'd gone away at eighteen to serve his country and then served in law enforcement. Baron, his dad, had always supported War's path but he'd been ready to hand over the gavel when War came back. If he knew half the stuff Baron and the guys would get up to, he would have set some ground rules.

He walked in and stared. Out of all the things he imagined, two high school boys he recognized from the football team hanging from the ceiling in their underwear weren't what he expected.

"Somebody want to explain what's going on?"

He was proud of himself at how calm he sounded but honestly this seemed small potatoes to some of the incidents lately.

Baron pointed at Rascal, Bear's dad, and he lowered one of the boys a little.

"Tell him why you're hanging from my ceiling," Baron grunted with a glare.

"I don't know why."

War catalogued the boy's eyes shifting to the left and up. War walked closer until his face was in front of the boy's.

"Well, then tell me this. How old are you?"

War waited. Whoever this was wouldn't win against him in the waiting game. He'd once sat silently in an interrogation room for forty minutes until the suspect couldn't handle the silence any longer.

"Eighteen."

Not a boy, an adult. He'd been surprised when he walked in because the Bluff Creek Brotherhood MC had stringent guidelines to protect children and those unable to help themselves. For him to be strung up, he'd guess Baron had deemed it a big offense.

"Somebody tell me what is going on. Now!"

"We got a call from a mother in town. Her daughter had been *bothered*," Baron air quoted the word, "and she didn't think the sheriff would deem it a big enough offense. The punks before us had done it to one of her friends earlier in the week. I just decided we'd see how they liked someone messing with their clothes and touching them without their consent."

"What exactly did you do?" His glare as he talked would have most men spilling their secrets. "Tell me and I'll consider how we'll deal with you."

The punk's eyes widened, and War looked behind him to see his mom had joined them.

"Ma'am, help me. They're hurting me."

His mom walked closer.

"You don't want me to help you. I've heard what you did. I don't like boys who think they have the right to do what they want because they're bigger or stronger than someone else. When someone says no, you need to listen. I'm sure my boys will figure out a way to teach it to you."

His mom turned and headed for the kitchen. Between her and Baron, he'd learned how a woman was supposed to be treated. These boys didn't seem to understand that.

"I'm feeling magnanimous today and I don't want someone to have to clean up blood before tonight's party. I'm going to let you walk back to town. The two-mile walk without shoes should help you think about consequences. I'll graciously allow you to keep your underwear. On the walk back, you can think about how the Bluff Creek Brotherhood MC is giving you a second chance to change your ways. You will not accept any rides offered. If someone asks why you're walking, you will say you're doing penance. No more or less. You will not do anything to anyone that they don't want. My brothers and I will all be keeping eyes on you. Don't confuse my mercy for weakness. Are we clear?"

At their nods, Baron and Rascal lowered them and untied them. Bear walked over, grabbing an arm of each and pulling them toward the door.

"I'll escort them to the edge of the property."

He looked each of the originals in the eyes. Not one of them had any remorse and honestly, he couldn't fault them. He'd quit the police force because he was tired of the victims never getting justice. Today, they'd scared the offenders and hopefully made it safer for the ladies to walk home.

"Can I trust you three to notify the girl's parents that we want to know if anything else happens?"

Their grins had him wondering if they'd set this up to test how he'd respond. He was sure the punks had taken liberties they shouldn't, but their usual response was to go to the punks' home and have a chat. Today had been a little different.

"Sure, Prez."

"Good job, War."

"You got it."

He shook his head as their words flew all at once. He was going to grab a beer, go finish reading the reports, and then hope someone at the party intrigued him. If he was lucky, the originals would man the grill tonight and stay out of trouble, but he wasn't counting on it. He'd been thrilled to be back in Bluff Creek and take over the MC but he wasn't sure how the hell he was going to deal with the originals. Most of them had been favored uncles growing up. They'd been the first good men he and his twin had come in contact with. Thank goodness he'd been out of diapers when he came so he didn't have them having that to throw in his face.

Chapter Two

Remington walked down the street to the entrance of the clubhouse. Winnie's words were ringing in her ears. *Are you sure you're up to this?* Was she up to this? She didn't have a choice. She was the one that was texting with their skip, and he was going to be at the Bluff Creek Brotherhood's Saturday night get together. The skip had been cagey when she'd messaged him on Facebook but after a couple days of her chatting and convincing him she wasn't a threat, he'd asked her to come to the party. He'd wanted to meet "Tonya" in person. She had a couple different names she used when hunting and Tonya had seemed just his type.

She'd been to the Bluff Creek Brotherhood compound and parties multiple times over the years, but she'd avoided it the last three months since Warrick Shields had come back. She actually preferred calling him the name he was called when he was younger because it irritated him so much. He didn't look like Ricky anymore. He was all man now, but she couldn't think about that. She needed to keep her mind on her job tonight. Lack of concentration bred mistakes, and mistakes in her business could mean lives lost.

Skirting her way into the clubhouse, she looked for tonight's loser. He'd mentioned he would be helping at the inside bar until eight, which worked perfectly. She'd wait until eight to walk in. She'd chat for a little bit, and they could hang out after he was done. Once he was comfortable, she'd take him out to the street off the MC property and her sisters would arrive to take him in. No big deal. Roam wouldn't think twice about seeing her hanging around and wouldn't do more than wave, so she'd only need to avoid War. She'd clocked him hanging outside and had taken the long way into the clubhouse. He'd been lounging against the table manning the bonfire. She'd been drawn to his strong jaw with his scruffy beard—not too long, just enough to rub against her neck and other interesting parts. He'd tried to look relaxed with his legs crossed at the ankle, but it was deceptive. He'd been scanning the area for threats. Jeans, motorcycle boots, a t-shirt, and his Bluff Creek Brotherhood cut had never looked so good on a man.

She'd worked to ensure she didn't catch his attention but his eyes following her let her know she'd failed. She should have chosen strappy sandals instead of her motorcycle boots but if she had to chase her mark, she didn't want to be in heels. She hated them. She couldn't understand how anyone could want to wear them.

As the oldest of the Franks sisters, she'd grown up babysitting her younger sisters, watching out for them, and now making sure they all came home alive. On a skip, it took seconds for things to turn from sugar to shit. Sometimes she wished everything didn't all hang on her shoulders. Her dad was looking to her and her sisters to take over Franks and Daughters Bail Bonds. She loved the business, yet occasionally, she dreamed about someone taking care of her. It probably came from too many princess movies growing up where the prince always rescued the princess. She didn't need rescuing, but she wouldn't turn down a shoulder to lean on. Of course, Ricky Shields had ruined princess movies for her. They were in high school, and his parents were throwing a big party at the MC. She'd been watching Matt and Ricky for years. For some reason, even though they were twins, she couldn't care less about Matt. Ricky drew her in even though he gave her no indication he saw her.

She'd decided to try to get his attention. She'd noticed the girls he gave attention to at school, so she'd decided she'd put a little effort in before they went to the party. She'd curled her thick hair though she usually wore it straight and found a cute skirt and shoes, even though she was far happier in jeans and motorcycle boots.

She'd barely walked in when Ricky had thrown a ball at Matt. Matt hadn't been watching and it had bounced off his shoulder, hitting the open bottles of soda on the table and knocking them over. She'd been standing by the table. The pop had drenched her shirt and skirt. When he'd smarted off and called her a princess, she'd run toward him to punch him. Her dad stopped her before she could do any damage. Ricky had been the bane of her existence after that, calling her princess every chance he got.

She'd convinced herself while he'd been gone that she'd left her animosity in the past. She'd fooled herself because she had a burning need to have him see the real her even though it was a pipe dream. Her best hope was a working relationship where she refrained from beating the crap out of him.

She forced a smile on her face as she spotted Kenny. She had a job to do and reminiscing over her high school crush wasn't going to get it done. Kenny wasn't the first slime ball she'd had to get close to and he wouldn't be the last.

War glanced around the picnic area, scanning for threats. Saturday nights had been a tradition for the Bluff Creek Brotherhood MC since his dad, Baron, and Regina had married. They opened it up to any townspeople who wanted to attend. Most people believed it was just a party. Baron, and now War as president, and the MC used it to check on everyone and check for new members. War noticed a couple new faces. He wasn't sure if they were hangarounds or new to town. Thank goodness Baron, Rascal, and Locks were occupied with the grills.

Over the years, Baron acquired more land until Bluff Creek Brotherhood MC was a small community. The compound sat on 640 acres but only part of it was fenced in. The gun range and tactical center along with the mechanics shop were in the secondary gated area, which was outside the gated compound. The MC didn't want people visiting the gun range to have access to the compound where they lived. When the gun range, shop, etc. were open, then the main gate to that area was open. The locals in the small town supported BCB. Having their town safe was worth a lot.

He was happy to be back, but he'd underestimated what being president entailed. Between all their different businesses, the paperwork alone was time-consuming. Even three months in, he'd only scratched the surface, but he couldn't imagine being anywhere else.

He'd missed his family and if he was being truthful with himself, he was ready to settle down. He'd never thought he'd be forty-three and unattached. He'd envisioned serving in the Army, working for a while in the police department, then coming home to the MC. He'd always figured he'd find his one. The woman who he couldn't live without. He couldn't imagine having anything less than what he'd grown up seeing with Baron and Regina. They were still as much in love today as they were when they met forty years ago.

Scoop walked over and motioned to a couple by the fire.

"War, you recognize them?"

War knew the hang-around who was working the bar tonight, but he didn't recognize the woman. He wouldn't mind getting to know her. Tight shorts highlighting a firm rounded ass leading down to thick thighs. Her hair reached a little below her shoulders. When she bent toward the man, her shirt rode up, exposing a strip of skin with a hint of a tattoo peeking out of her shorts. Her hand slid through her hair, pulling it back. Mirrored sunglasses obscured her face, but he'd caught a partial glimpse of her profile before she reached and grasped the man's hand. She tugged him toward her as she walked backwards.

He was on the shorter side with quite the gut hanging over his belt. In his forties, War wasn't as fit as when he was younger but he and the guys all kept in shape. Sure, his abs had a little more flesh over his six-pack, but he wasn't bursting over his belt.

The woman giggled and slipped her arm under his, leaning her head on his shoulder. She was hot. His first look at her face had him spellbound. Dark red full lips spread in a smile had him wanting to go closer. He stood and followed at a distance. She intrigued him and he hadn't felt that in too long. They meandered through the cars with her working to keep his hands off her breasts.

If she was so interested, why was she evading his touch? Something was off here, and his senses were telling him things weren't as they seemed.

She brushed her ear as they reached the edge of the parking lot. She tugged him out the gates and closer to the street. What was she doing? There were a couple cars parked on the road, but they'd tried to keep everyone off the black top. They had a farmer across the way who routinely drove his tractor on the road.

The man reached for her face as an SUV skidded to a stop beside them. In seconds, two others piled out of the car and had him handcuffed on the ground. All but the woman from the party were wearing vests which said FUGITIVE RECOVERY AGENT.

"Everything okay here?"

The brunette who'd led the man out to the team turned and grinned. "It's peachy. We're just taking out some trash." She slid her glasses up on her head.

He smirked at her tone. Up close, he catalogued her features. She was even more beautiful from the front. Full, lush lips. Gorgeous brown eyes which reminded him of the sunflowers his mother grew. Bustline which was curvy but not her main feature. No, he loved her full thighs and full butt.

"I appreciate that. Who should I thank for the disposal?"

"Franks and Daughters Bail Bonds."

Oh, this was too good. She hadn't recognized him but then he'd changed a lot, too. Who knew his little pest back in high school had turned into such a hot woman who he'd love to get closer to? She'd been pretty in high school but off limits even though he'd been tempted. Now she ignited a flame only she could put out.

"Hey, Princess, maybe I could take you out and thank you in person?"

She glared. Maybe he was wrong, and she'd known who he was already. Either way, it didn't matter. Ticking her off might be his new favorite hobby.

"No thanks needed. Just doing our job, but we need to go and get him dropped off. Besides, it looks like the road name and becoming president hasn't improved your personality any. I'm not your friggin' princess, Ricky. Things have changed and I'm happy to go a couple rounds in the ring if you can't remember what to call me."

Climbing in the passenger seat, she tapped the dash. The driver smiled and waved, then backed into the driveway to turn.

Who knew Remington had turned into such a badass? Although his nickname for her had certainly garnered a reaction. He hoped Roam hadn't imbibed too much but his kids were being watched by a babysitter, so anything was possible. He needed to know everything about what had happened to Remington over the years, and he required the information immediately. She was feisty. Between her body and her temper, he had to adjust himself. Maybe his response would be a onetime deal because he didn't need to be getting any ideas about how Locks' oldest daughter would look lying naked on his bedspread or what he'd like to do to her.

He'd hoped she'd be married with kids so his mom wouldn't continue to bug him about them getting together but at least annoying her might provide some entertainment. He'd enjoyed getting a rise out of her in high school and nothing had changed. He only hoped his brother hadn't hit that while he was gone because they had a rule about dating each other's leftovers. Hell, with Remington, though, he'd be tempted to torpedo the rule.

Chapter Three

"Oh, Remi, I think you have an admirer in the Bluff Creek Brotherhood."

"Shut up, Beth."

"Whoa, I'm sensing a little animosity."

"I am, too. Did the Prez get under your skin, Remi? He couldn't take his eyes off you but then there was a lot of you showing tonight. More than I've seen in a while," Winnie teased.

"You know, I'm wishing I was an only child right about now."

"Eww, Rem, Win, I am deeply hurt. I always adored my big sister and she hurt my feelings saying she doesn't want us around."

"Beth, nobody wants your sarcasm right now." Remington wished she could go back a couple hours and have one of her sisters play bait for their prey. She'd known she'd be pushing it but, in her mind, she'd hoped he'd see how she'd matured and maybe decide he didn't need to tease her. She was irritated that she still cared what he thought.

Regina was probably ecstatic to have all her kids home. Baron had been ready for the next generation to run the MC and hadn't wasted any time passing the MC to War. Baron was still active, but they wanted time to be grandparents to Roam's kids. Honestly, the bitch leaving was probably best in the long run for Roam. She didn't use that word lightly, but his wife had been a piece of work. Jealous of everything. I guess when you trap your husband by getting pregnant, you always assumed everyone was out to take him. Roam was one of the sweetest men she knew. A complete opposite from his irritating twin. If only she could be attracted to him. She adored his kids. She and her sisters had helped with the kids a couple of times until his wife had said she didn't want their influence around. Her jealousy when she'd learned Roam had done a tattoo for her had been ridiculous. He was a genius with the tattoo gun. She only trusted him or Rascal to do her art. Each piece meant something to her, and no one was screwing it up.

The noise from her sisters' chattering was giving her a headache. They always had her back but sometimes, she wanted a little peace and quiet. Working with each other day in and day out made for a lot of sister time but also time to get on each other's nerves. Her dad had added on over the years to his compound to include houses for all of them as they got older. They all still met for breakfast in the main house and hung out but sometimes she needed a little calm plus she was a neat freak.

Being the closest in age, she and Sarah probably would have been best friends, but Winnie was the one she always turned to. She loved all her sisters, but she and Winnie could talk about anything. Winnie also knew how much Warrick had hurt her all those years ago. Her mom had understood but been practical. She'd told Remington boys would come and go and heartache was a fact of life. Winnie had been the one who held her in her room while she sobbed. It would have been so much easier to fall for Roam, but he was in the brother category. The thought of kissing him made her retch.

"Will you all shut up? You're giving me a headache and we have an hour of driving before we drop off Mr. 'I Forgot About My Bail Hearing.' How about a little peace and quiet?"

She twisted the top off the drink Beth handed her. Maybe some liquid would help her headache. Then she'd need to disinfect herself after they dropped him off. She felt so dirty having her arm around him and her shoulders smelled of BO from being under his arm. Yuck. The things she did to catch a skip. She loved her job, just not all aspects of it.

Last Spring, when they'd used the dogs to find the skip from Kansas City, she'd adored the thrill of the chase. Her dad had brought them up in the business. He'd never made them work for him but they'd each fallen in love with the job. As the oldest, she decided with her dad which people to bond out and also coordinated their team for retrievals of skips. She also met with any of their prospective security clients. It was a part of the business she'd suggested adding. Business was phenomenal. Having female bodyguards for some of their female clients allowed it to look like they were just shopping or out on the town blending in. She found it a nice break from chasing skips. Each of her sisters had jobs which played to their strengths. If she had to stay in the office all the time, she'd go crazy. Which reminded her, she hadn't checked in yet. Mr. Tall, Dark and Annoying had distracted her.

She hit one on her phone and waited.

"Yes?"

"Code Monica. An hour out from drop-off."

They'd all grown up watching *Friends* and had adopted their theme song as their own. When they had been reworking some things in the office, they'd come up with codes with their favorite characters. Code Monica meant everything was perfect and no injuries.

"No injuries except to Remi's ego. War was there!" Winnie yelled from the back seat.

Sarah giggled. "I'll wait for the report when you all get back."

"Thanks. See you in a couple."

She almost wished she'd stayed on the phone. Maybe if she concentrated on inconsequential things, she could wipe him from her mind.

At forty-three, she'd given up finding a man who could live with her lifestyle. Leaving at all hours of the night on a job stressed the relationship and being gone weeks at a time for a security gig wasn't conducive to dating. Her shooting better than ninety percent of the men she'd dated had been the nail in the coffin in most of her relationships. If they couldn't handle her being better than them, she wished them well and booted them out the door.

She longed to be like Winnie. As the third oldest, Winnie wasn't looking for Mr. Right. She was enjoying Mr. Right Now—then she'd move on when she became bored. After her latest dating fiasco, they couldn't even show themselves in their favorite bar in Dodge City. Winnie had dated all three of the brothers within a couple weeks of each other. Even though she wasn't dating them at the same time, they took offense to her moving on so quickly. Now they had to hang out somewhere else until it wasn't quite so fresh in their minds, which was inconvenient. She loved that bar. She could relax and let down her guard knowing the brothers who owned it would watch over them.

Too bad Warrick was such an ass, otherwise she'd consider taking him for a test drive. Who knew her nemesis could be such a turn on with his scruffy beard, toned arms and chest? Maybe if the right opportunity presented itself, she could take Tall, Dark and Built for a test drive because a lot of her books indicated hate sex was good and he certainly appeared as if he knew what he was doing. At six feet tall, she was the tallest of her siblings. Growing up at school dances, the boys' faces had always been in her breasts. How nice it would be to have to look up for a change. She'd estimate he was easily six foot four. He might even be able to lift her onto a counter and there were so many things she dreamed of doing on a counter.

"Okay, we're here. Rock, paper, scissors on who has to take him in?" Beth's hopeful voice pulled her out of her thoughts.

"Nope. You traded me four times of intake for the Keifer skip. You had plans," Winnie gleefully replied.

"I am really disappointed in you all," Beth sighed.

"Whatever. You made your bed now go enjoy Officer Handsy and his unrequited love. Jesse, it's your turn to accompany."

Beth got out grumbling underneath her breath, walking around to get Kenny. Beth was their glass half full type of person even when the glass was full of vinegar, but she despised taking in skips and dealing with how she was treated. She could always see the rainbow despite the rain. She was a lot like Winnie. Sunshine when the clouds and rain were overshadowing everything on the horizon.

Remi should have volunteered to go in. Now she was stuck in the car thinking. How the heck was she going to deal with having Warrick, or War as his cut said, around all the time? Her dad and their family had been invited to Sunday lunch at the MC for the last twenty years and she always went. Being out of town, she'd been looking forward to the food. Regina's cooking was a treat, and she wasn't sure she could give it up but being around him every week was not what she wanted.

Remi also missed just being around Regina. When they'd lost their mom ten years ago, everyone looked to Remi as the oldest daughter. Between all of them being grief-stricken, Regina had stepped in and been a sounding board for Remi. She didn't want to lose that relationship, but she also didn't want to come between War and his mom.

If she could get him to quit calling her princess, maybe she could deal with him. He was oh so easy on the eyes and she'd had a long dry spell. Maybe a one and done to scratch an itch. She could make sure his mouth was occupied so he didn't have a chance to call her princess.

"Hey, Remi, I know having him back is going to be hard. I'm here if you need to talk." Winnie's hand patted her shoulder. And that was why she loved her sisters. They could tease, torment, and beat up on each other but there was no one else she'd rather have at her back than them. Whether it was taking down a skip or having a shoulder to cry on because everything was falling apart, they'd always be there for each other.

Chapter Four

Remi rode alongside Winnie toward the Bluff Creek Clubhouse. She'd already decided she wasn't missing another Sunday dinner because of War, when her dad had stomped into her house. He rarely lost his temper, but he'd called her actions childish and instructed her all his daughters would be at lunch. She had no problem disagreeing with her dad when she was right, but she wasn't going to argue over lunch. She'd use it as an opportunity for War to see her as an adult. Hiding out for the last three months, taking any security job available, hadn't been the adult thing to do but she hadn't been ready to see him.

She had disagreed with riding with her dad. She didn't need to be crammed into the SUV. Winnie had jumped at the chance to ride with her. Sun and very little wind was an unusual day in Bluff Creek. Not having to fight the wind on the bike was very relaxing.

Pulling into their driveway, she and Winnie backed their bikes in, and she readied to deal with War. If all else failed, she'd invite him into the ring and maybe knock some sense into him. She wished things were different but his view of her was skewed. She wasn't a princess. She was a woman who didn't need someone trying to fit her into a little box. She was who she was and wasn't changing to fit some ideal some man had of her.

If he was the man she'd always wanted, he'd help her become more and complete her. He wouldn't need her to become less to fit his stringent ideals. Her mom had not only been a great mom, but she'd also been an integral part of the business. Her parents had grown the bail bonds company from just her dad and mom to over fifteen employees before she passed. With her sisters' input into the company, they now had offices in Topeka and Wichita along with Bluff Creek. Her idea to partner with the MC for the security arm of the company was set to hit six figures in revenue in the first eighteen months. She loved the intricacies and variations to her job, but she still dreamed of having it all—a job she loved and a family with a man who loved and adored her.

Walking in, she spotted Roam with his little ones and the guys crowded around. Why she couldn't be attracted to him instead of his twin War was annoying. Although he'd grown up as Matt or Matty to her, he'd been Roam for so long that she couldn't imagine calling him anything else.

One of the things she loved about being in the clubhouse was how the men were all family oriented. Rascal had already commandeered Casper. Bear, who she hadn't seen in forever, almost showed a little smile while he was holding Georgia. Rascal had been waiting for him to come home. He'd even tried to talk with her about whether she'd ever had a crush on Bear in school. He was wanting grandbabies and thought she might be interested.

He'd been coined Bear when he was in middle school. He was always thinking through the worst-case scenarios. From a tactical standpoint, she loved that and had already texted with him about helping with the security company. Since she had to explain the company to him, she assumed Baron hadn't shared it was a joint venture between the MC and the bail bonds company. She couldn't wait to be War's boss on one of the security details. Bossing him around could be her new favorite pastime.

Roam's oldest, Grant, saw her and immediately scrambled to get out of War's arms.

"Memi!" he screeched, running with his arms up.

"Have you missed me?" She giggled as she acted like she was munching on his neck.

He leaned back and placed his hands along her cheeks. Oh, she knew where he was going with this. He was already a heartbreaker with his long lashes and blue eyes. "Memi, vroom?"

"Were you good while I was gone?"

His exaggerated nod almost knocked her in the chin. "If I ask your daddy, would he say you've been good?" He paused, peeking underneath his lashes to see if Roam was close. He only did that when he'd gotten in trouble. She couldn't wait to hear the story. Grant was like a little monkey climbing on everything. A couple months ago, right after they'd moved in, he'd shoved his little table and chairs close to the cabinet to climb up on the counter. Regina had said no more cookies until after supper. When she'd gone to do laundry, he'd decided he wanted more. Roam had been adventurous, too, growing up so it's not like he could blame anyone but himself. He finally nodded slowly.

"I be good." His smile was mischievous, but she wasn't his mom, so she wasn't going to call him on it.

"Okay, here's your present. It's a 1970 GTO this time."

He grasped the car, smacked a wet kiss on her cheek and shook to be put down.

"Daddy, lookie!" he screamed.

Her stomach churned at the thought of dealing with War. She bypassed the large table and chairs set up in the middle, heading toward the bathroom. Maybe running cold water on her wrists would help her calm down. Why did he have to affect her so much and why did she still care what he thought of her? She wanted him to see her as a strong, capable woman. His digs about her being a princess hit at the heart of her ego. She could take care of herself and quite well. She didn't need rescued.

"Lunch, everyone!"

She loved Regina but she wished lunch would have taken longer. Maybe she could sit as far away as possible. The Sunday lunch group was large with all the MC, her family, and Regina invited any of the bail bonds or security company employees also. She should have made a plan with her sisters before lunch to sit on both sides of her and across from her. Not that she needed protection, but a buffer zone would be great.

Glancing around the table without meeting anyone's eyes, she considered faking an illness. The only freaking seat still open was across from War and between Bear and another MC guy she didn't know. Thank goodness, Regina had made fried chicken. At least she'd have good food. Settling into her seat, she made it a point to not look across from her. She'd gotten the whole looking beside or through someone down to a fine art with her security work. If only she could leave her sunglasses on at the table.

Baron sat at the head of the table with Regina beside him. Noah, her dad, or Locks as the MC called him, was on the other side. Baron said a blessing and then the clatter of dishes being emptied filled the space. Bear handed her the platter of chicken with a nudge.

"Please note, I only took one drumstick since I know that's your favorite."

She giggled. She didn't freaking giggle, but she'd completely forgotten the drumstick incident. Bear was pessimistic on a good day but downright grumpy on most days. She'd taken the last drumstick off the plate and passed the chicken to him. Of course, Regina always fixed more than one chicken, but he'd assumed it was the last one. If she remembered right, they'd been in high school. He'd really wanted the drumstick and had immediately started offering her things. First, it had been a free oil change. She'd replied with she changed her own oil. Her dad had taught all the sisters vehicle maintenance. He'd then offered more things and she turned each down. She'd been interested in how far he would go. He'd finally offered to give her lessons on bike maintenance. She'd been saving to buy her own bike, but her dad said no motorcycles at the house besides his unless they knew how to take care of it. He hadn't had time in his schedule to teach her. She'd said yes, handed him her drumstick, then walked in the kitchen and grabbed one from the extra chicken Regina had been warming in the oven. She'd never seen his face so red, but he'd stuck to the bargain. A couple months of lessons and she'd been able to buy her motorcycle.

He'd given her way more than the drumstick was worth so a couple months later after she'd saved her money up, she'd bought him the special saddlebags he'd been wanting. She'd enjoyed being around Bear despite his grumpiness. She sometimes wondered if it was more than grumpiness, but she'd never suggested it could be depression. Bear was like a brother. She wished she could think of him as more instead of being attracted to the jackass sitting across from her.

"Oh yeah, our princess always had to have the food she wanted."

War's tone had her hackles rising but she was sticking to the plan and not letting him bait her.

"Dang, brother, the city teach you to be a jackass?"

She didn't want to cause dissension between Roam and War, but she appreciated him standing up for her. She'd defuse the situation and not give an argument a chance to brew. She was on her best behavior today.

"Not a princess but anybody who says they don't have a favorite of Regina's fried chicken is lying, and the mashed potatoes and gravy...nobody makes it like Regina. Thanks for fixing the meal."

A chorus of voices echoing her sentiments distracted the group from War's words. She turned toward the man on her right.

"Hi, I don't believe we've met. I'm Remington."

He wiped his mouth, adjusting his glasses. "Scoop. Nice to meet you."

"Scoop? Like ice cream?" Sarah asked from across the table.

He blushed a little, adjusting his glasses again. "Umm, no. I do tech work. Finding data about individuals."

"Nice. That's what I do for the bail bonds company, Rocky Road," Sarah sassed.

She didn't care what Sarah called Scoop as long as all eyes weren't on her, and she wasn't listening to War call her princess again. If he'd keep his mouth shut, she could enjoy and appreciate the man War had grown into. As a senior in high school, he'd been cute but now, he was swoon worthy. Angular jaw covered by a closely trimmed beard. A tight white t-shirt underneath his cut hugged what she could see of his chest. He was a little thicker around the waist, but he was someone she'd take home if she saw him in a bar. His arms with the tattoos just begged to have her tongue tracing them. She glanced up and his eyes caught her checking him out. His lips quirked in a smirk. She'd love to be kissing them but then he'd freaking open his mouth and irritate her.

"Like what you see, Princess?"

His words were soft enough only those directly beside them heard. Sarah paused as did Winnie across the table. They both knew she had a temper. She did quite well holding her temper and putting up with a lot on jobs but sometimes, she was pushed too far and then exploded. War was tramping on her last nerve.

"You've been gone a long time. I was seeing the difference in you. I figured there were changes and since you're the president of the MC, I'd hoped you'd kept in shape. You don't look bad, and I was cataloguing where I could use you."

"Where you could use me? What are you talking about?" he growled.

"At Bluff Creek Security."

She was being short on purpose. She was enjoying him not knowing about their partnership. His dismayed look was too good to miss out on.

"What the hell is Bluff Creek Security?"

"It's a subdivision on the bail bonds company but it's a joint venture between the MC and the bail bonds. In the short time it's been open, it's already shown how lucrative it will be. We're all excited about the possibilities." Roam grabbed a roll and calmly started buttering it as he finished.

"Princess, why the hell would you think you'd decide where you could use me?" he grunted.

"Because it was her idea along with Beth and she heads the division. Do you have a problem with a woman being in charge?" Regina snapped as she stood and glared at her son.

Remi was ecstatic she'd come to lunch. She'd been worried about him, but it seemed today was going to be fun. War was showing his chauvinism and Regina wasn't having any of it. This was way more fun than she'd imagined. She sipped her tea, waiting for what he'd say next. War may be an ass to her, but she couldn't fault him as a son. He adored his mother and would do anything for her. She was almost giddy waiting to see how he dug himself out of this one.

"I don't have a problem with a woman being in charge. I, um, think women are great."

Laughter flowed around the table as the brothers lost it.

"Smooth." Bear, who rarely smiled, was grinning.

"You don't have a problem with a woman being in charge or you actively support a woman leading? There's a difference, War. I didn't raise you to act like this, especially with family."

If it wasn't too obvious, she'd pull her phone out to video. His pleading look toward his brothers to help him out would provide so much enjoyment when she was bored on a job. His attitude toward her was understandable. They'd always been like oil and water after he was a jerk, but even though it killed her to admit it—he was a good man.

She was fanatical about puzzles. It's one of the things that made her awesome at her job. She dug until she got down to the heart of an issue whether it was chasing someone down or figuring out from their habits where they'd run to. War was different from when he left. It was puzzling and she'd never been able to leave a puzzle alone until she'd figured it out. War just moved to the top of her list of people to research. Of course, she'd have to keep it secret, or she'd never hear the end of it from her sisters.

Chapter Five

How did lunch go downhill so fast? He'd asked a question, albeit a little harshly and suddenly, he was in his mom's crosshairs being cross-examined by a master. Three months home and everything was going awesome until Remington Franks walked back in. He'd deal with Remington later but right now, he needed to make this right with his mom.

"I apologize, Mom. I was caught off guard about the security business and didn't realize Remington was in charge. I have no problem working for a woman if she's capable."

Bear shook his head at him. What the hell? His answer was a good enough non-answer that he didn't have to actively support Remington, per se, but he supported other women in leadership and apologized to his mom. He'd been a detective and could be diplomatic when he needed to be—not that he should have to be in his own MC clubhouse. He was the president, which meant Remington should report to him, or they should at least be on equal footing if the security business was a partnership.

His mom was still giving him the glare and he knew he wasn't out of the woods yet.

"Hey, Remington, why don't you show him how capable you are? Sounds like he needs a little convincing, but you both have to wear gloves and headgear. We have the meeting for that month-long contract tomorrow," Winnie suggested.

Remington's middle sister had always been the instigator and today wasn't any different. She wanted him to fight Remington. He'd had to practice with women police officers at the academy and years ago, he'd sparred with his first female partner. He shook his head. He didn't need those thoughts in his head right now.

He hoped his dad or mom would put a stop to this. Maybe with that reasoning, they shouldn't be fighting after Sunday lunch but by the looks on their faces, they weren't coming to his rescue.

"I'm a little full from this amazing lunch. Maybe some other time."

Was she scared to fight him? She seemed so different from the girl he knew in high school who was upset they'd spilled punch on her dress. He'd felt bad when he'd thrown the football and been embarrassed. He'd smarted off and she'd been so mad, their dads had to pull them apart. Before that she'd always been one of the Franks daughters. She'd been more of a jeans and motorcycle boots person. She and Matt had always gotten along but she'd rubbed him the wrong way. He wasn't interested in going in the ring with her, though he'd do it to save face. He'd take the reprieve she offered. He needed to know more about her before he got in the ring. He didn't want to do something to completely screw up what sounded like a lucrative business for the MC.

"I agree. I'm full and I'm looking forward to apple cobbler."

He imagined the relief he saw on Remington's face was reflected on his. He was sure he could beat her, but he didn't need to tick her off when they might be working together. He had no problem beating up on his brother and the other brothers who had knowledge of it for not mentioning the security company and Remington's involvement. That seemed like something that should have come up in their weekly meetings these last couple of months. He was interested in what exactly the security company provided. War finished lunch and then decided to go on a ride. He needed space from everyone. Taking to the road was always a place he thought best and being back around everyone had him needing space.

After riding for a couple hours, he pulled over near the creek. He had a lot of memories along here. Baron had taught them to swim at this creek. He and Roam had ridden dirt bikes along the hills nearby. He hadn't realized how much things had changed. The last couple of months had been an adjustment. Being away for so long, he'd created an idyllic view of home. He'd known people would have grown older, but his view was of the past. He'd thought he and the guys coming home would be the ones to change everything—make the MC all it could be. Half the things he'd envisioned had already been added in the last few years—the gun range and tactical center for one. His dad and the brothers over the years had set the groundwork for the future. Coming home was more about how he and his friends fit into the MC and how they could help grow it in the years to come. He wished there was a roadmap of how to navigate the MC he'd come home to.

He wasn't the only one whose vision had been stuck in the past. He loved his parents and the MC, but he'd forgotten how everyone was in everyone else's business. His mom vacillated between treating him as a man and the president of the club and then bossing him around as if he was still in high school. He was treading a tightrope with the originals, too. They had a huge amount of wisdom he gave due consideration to but ultimately, he was leading. His dad had handed over the president's gavel but was still a member. And the freaking life questions as if getting married and having kids was a given. He'd lost track of the times someone had asked him when he was going to settle down. The funniest one had to be Bear. He'd understood when Bear had done it because Regina had been trying to ask him what he wanted in a woman so she could help him find someone since she knew all the available women. Bear had not only thrown him under the bus by deflecting to War's single status but had driven the bus back over him when he suggested Regina should work on helping him first since he was older. He hadn't figured out how he was paying him back for getting Regina's laser focus targeted on him, but he was sure something appropriate would come to him.

If he and Remington weren't at each other's throats all the time, he could see himself with her. Even when she was pissing him off, he was so turned on he had to work on hiding it. She was the only one appearing in his dreams and most nights, she was who he pictured when he took things in hand. He hadn't even had a blow job since he'd seen her at the party. No one interested him like she did.

Even when she was tramping on his last nerve, he admired her. She was capable and Locks would never have put her in charge if she couldn't handle it. He wondered how he'd react to her if they didn't have their history.

When he pictured himself with someone, she would be the type of woman he pictured. A woman who knew the score. He didn't want to have to wonder if she could handle their lifestyle. Roam had talked non-stop about how if it wasn't for Remington, he wasn't sure if the bail bonds company would have survived. When Remington's mom had died ten years ago, Locks had been devastated and ignored the business for a while. Remington had held the family together while keeping the bail bonds company from going under. Now he found out she'd also added a joint security company which was profitable. Maybe she wasn't the princess he'd grown up with. She'd grown up close to the MC. Locks had kept some distance until their bail bonds company was established. Remington was exactly the kind of woman he was attracted to; gorgeous, strong, and smart. He also wanted to protect his woman and he wasn't sure Remington would ever allow a man close enough to protect her and shield her from the storms of life. In his mind, the man was the ultimate head of the household, and his woman would need to understand that. She'd also have to know he couldn't tell her everything. Baron had always protected his mom and it was the kind of relationship he aspired to.

Life was more complicated than he'd imagined. If he could present a calm façade while dealing with his corrupt chief, then surely he'd be able to adjust his attitude and work for the security company for the good of his MC. Maybe he and Remington could even work together. He grabbed his phone and contemplated how to word a text. He could adjust his attitude, but he wasn't going to overthink every little word. Since they would be working together, they'd need to learn to read each other.

War: Could we meet? I'll buy lunch and we can discuss which men to schedule for security.

He waited for a reply, watching the dots for what seemed like forever. How hard could it be to say yes or no? He'd hoped they could work together but not because he wanted to be around her. He didn't want his mom thinking less of him.

Remi: Per protocols, we don't meet to decide who is available. I assign who best fits the case. If there is a valid reason why they can't, we consider changing. I appreciate you wanting input but like I said—not protocol.

So, basically, he was at the mercy of whatever she wanted. Maybe he was wrong wanting to appease his mom. He was president and that counted for something. Little Miss Princess needed to get on board and remember who he was. Why was he the one who had to do all the changing? Why couldn't she bend a little? Maybe she still was the little princess he'd thought, only playing at being an adult. He wasn't putting up with her shit.

War: It is now, Princess.

He laid his phone down, breathing deep and tapping his hand. He wanted to go hit something. Why did every conversation with Remington end up with him furious? He really needed to go blow off some steam and hit something. He glanced at the phone, but Remington hadn't replied. He'd tried to do something nice, and it had backfired. He wasn't sure what he'd do next, but he was positive he was staying away from his mom just in case Remington tattled on him.

He headed over to change clothes. He'd go throw some punches at someone then maybe check with the guys to see if anyone wanted to play poker. He needed something to distract him.

Chapter Six

Remington had tried to let War continuing to call her princess slide off but today was not that day. His text last week demanding to be included in who she scheduled had irritated her. She'd ignored his last text of *It is now, Princess* even though she wanted to tell him to kiss her ass.

Then today happened. Every single thing that could go wrong had. A client's final payment had been rejected by the bank for insufficient funds. Normally, she wouldn't have had to deal with it but since she was meeting about when he needed them next month, accounting had punted it to her. When she questioned the client, it was all she could do to not grab his neck and squeeze. He was going through a divorce and had declared bankruptcy so he wouldn't have to pay her. He was so sure they'd give him extra time to pay. She wouldn't be protecting a weasel who was trying to hide money from his wife and four kids. In fact, she was seriously considering offering the wife and kids their help and protection free of charge. She hated men who let their children suffer all to make a point.

She'd headed for her next meeting in the next county over, only to arrive and get a text the client was canceling. Then, this icing on her shitastic day. War had decided she must not know her own mind and decided to text again three days after the first time.

War: Have you thought any more about meeting regarding the schedule?

No, she hadn't thought any more about them meeting because she was honestly worried what she'd do if she saw him in person. How could she be so attracted to someone she wanted to climb him like a tree and let him have her against a wall but at the same time, envision using him for target practice at the range? She'd been more confused in the last week than in her whole life. Every time she dreamed about a man, War's face and voice were who she pictured. Of course, in her dreams, he wasn't the ass he was in person. His gruff voice wasn't telling her what to do. It was telling her to scream his name when she came. She didn't know what his touch felt like but, in her dreams, she couldn't get enough of him.

She didn't know why she'd imagined him saying he was too full at lunch so they didn't fight was actually his attitude turning a corner. If he thought because he was now the president, they'd be changing their working protocols, he was incorrect. He could request a change to the contract. All their protocols and how to change them between the two entities had been spelled out months ago because she was a businesswoman who knew her shit. Their agreement wasn't at the whim of the president, it was a business contract.

Remi: I'm busy. I will email you the schedule. End of discussion.

Maybe that would shut him up. She didn't need to keep dealing with this. Did he not realize she ran the freaking company? Sure, her dad was a huge part of it, but she was in charge. It was all on her shoulders, and she didn't have time to deal with holding his freaking hand. Though once in a while, she wished for someone to discuss everything with. Someone who she could chat about her day with.

WAR

War: Listen, Princess. We need to find a way to work together so you need to make time for me.

Oh, she did, did she? His resorting to calling her princess again instead of dealing with this like adults rubbed her the wrong way. Though if he wasn't such an ass, she might consider letting him rub her in all the right ways. It was a nice twist of fate she was in Dodge City and could drop by the party store. Little Ricky Shields needed to be taught a lesson. If he was going to call her princess, then she'd call him by his childhood name, too. She knew exactly how she was going to get her point across. She'd grab some supplies and let her sisters know *Code Rachel* tonight. Time to take care of Mr. Ricky Warrick Shields once and for all. Although *Code Rachel* usually meant need emotional backup—no questions asked, she was sure her sisters would be willing to support her in anything. A small clandestine op tonight would help him remember she and her sisters were strong, capable women and he'd better not call her a princess again. He'd learn to appreciate who she was now or suffer the consequences.

Remington parked the SUV a half mile away from the clubhouse on the dirt road and hopped out, going to the back to grab their supplies. She'd known her sisters wouldn't let her down and in a couple of hours, they'd had everything together. They'd only been waiting for it to get dark enough to sneak across the field.

"I know this is a little more than a *Code Rachel* usually involves," she whispered.

"Honestly, I'm surprised one of us didn't add this on in high school. We missed so much not getting back at some of those asinine high school boys," Beth replied.

Sarah pulled her backpack out and shrugged it on. "I agree. I would have been so much happier if instead of just commiserating over my jackass date on prom night, we had done something to get him back."

Remi stepped slowly across the field. They didn't want to use flashlights and catch anyone's attention. When they came to the MC fence, Winnie scaled it and dropped to the other side, unlatching the gate. She smiled at the fact they were using the entrance she knew Bear had brought up multiple times to have them change and make secure. He'd explained no matter how easy it made getting equipment in, it wasn't safe because it couldn't be seen from the clubhouse. She was sure they'd be changing that after they saw what she'd done.

Crouching down, she glanced to where the motorcycles were usually parked by the clubhouse. It was empty, which was perfect for her. The building they parked in during bad weather wasn't used for anything else and had a crappy lock on it. They assumed no one would come on a biker compound and steal stuff. And she wasn't. She was just going to do a little decorating of War's bike and remind him she didn't appreciate him calling her princess.

As a biker herself, she'd never actually hurt someone's bike, but she could dress it up a little. Jesse picked the lock on the side of the building, and they walked in.

"Okay, I'll keep watch. There aren't any windows for light to shine through so you can use your flashlights. Three minutes then we're out of here," Sarah instructed.

Beth opened the pack and held up the items. Remi grabbed the pink heels first and slid one on the kickstand while Winnie held the bike steady. Then she took the other and placed it on the seat with a crown around it.

Winnie pulled a package out of her pocket, handing it to her. She hated glitter but for War, she'd use it. She opened the packet and sprinkled it all over the bike. Taking the streamers, she attached them to his handlebars. Then she took the keychains she'd had made with the high heel, crown, and the words *not your friggin princess* and hung them on his side mirrors, tag and anywhere else she could find. Jesse waited for Remi and everyone to step away from the bike before opening the two bags of filled balloons and dumping them around the bike. One last large sign propped against the front of the tire and they were done.

"Let's go," Sarah whispered.

Remi gave one last glance then snapped a quick picture of her work. Hopefully this would send him the message she wasn't his princess, and he wasn't in charge. If not, she had lots of ideas on how to get her point across. His name may be War but he'd rue the day he decided to be an ass.

Chapter Seven

War sipped his cup of coffee waiting for the guys to come in. Council was in ten minutes and he had a long list of everything he wanted to discuss. After lunch when he found out there were parts of the MC business he didn't even know about, he'd asked questions and spent time trying to figure out what all he was in charge of. He wasn't done by any means, but he'd identified most of the businesses.

Maybe he'd give Gage a call. His youngest brother had chosen to be a part of their Texas chapter. When he heard Gage was going to prospect there, he'd understood. Gage hadn't gone into the military. He'd wanted to prospect after high school but he'd believed the old timers might not see him as an adult. Although the Texas chapter knew Gage, they hadn't bandaged his scraped knees or taught him to ride a bike. War understood wanting to make your own way. Chatting with Gage might give him insight and he missed his brother. Maybe a trip to Texas was in order, too. A six-hour ride would be a great way to think and relax.

Where the hell was everybody? They were never late for council unless it was an emergency. He didn't hear any gunshots or see any blood, so they better have a good excuse for disrespecting him and his office.

Bear peeked his head in. "Hey, you need to come see this."

He followed Bear out, wondering what he had to see and why it was disrupting his meeting. The garage door where he'd parked his bike last night was open. Everyone was gathered around, and most were taking pictures and videos. Laughter and jeers had him pushing through to see.

"Didn't know you were into high heels, brother."

"I'm not sure we can keep you as president if pink's your new signature color."

His brothers' words flying at him had him curious. His first glimpse had him clenching his hands and trying to contain his temper. He had no doubt he could blame Remington for the decorations on his bike. He hoped she was ready for what she unleashed. He'd tried to be a little nicer in deference to his mom but screwing with his bike was war. He didn't get his name for being a pushover.

The heel on his kickstand had him ready to scream. Seriously, a pink heel! He'd never hear the end of this. He needed to get their minds off his bike and on to something else. He'd figure out a way to get her back later, and he would be getting her back.

"Glad you all find this so funny. It shows a glaring opening in our defenses if she can get on our property and deface my bike." He glared at each of them. A couple had the decency to look down. Baron patted him on the back.

"Way to deflect. You and Remington need to come to a cease fire. We've always had a good working relationship with them."

War kept his cool, but his dad's words irritated him. How the hell was it his fault Remington did this to his bike? It's like his dad wasn't even looking at the fact she and most likely her sisters had broken into the garage. He'd get her back, but he'd have to do it in a way Baron wouldn't find out. He'd take his time and figure it out. Anticipation of the payback was half the fun.

"Let's get inside. You're all late to council."

They'd meet for council and then he'd start researching. There had to be something in her past to exploit. He didn't want to cause any harm, but he wouldn't mind pissing off the little princess and showing her who was boss.

With trying to get a handle on running the MC, he needed to be devoting his time to improving their money flow and looking at increasing their members. Remington was a distraction he didn't need but he would not allow her disrespect to him, and his bike, to go unpunished. He was the president of Bluff Creek Brotherhood MC, and she would show him the respect afforded him. If he allowed her to disrespect him, what would that say to the new brothers when they came in?

What he'd really like to do was spank her butt for disrespecting him then spend the next few hours exploring her curves. Why did he have to be attracted to the woman who jumped on his last nerve? Why couldn't he take what some of the women who visited the compound so readily offered? Each time one of them came on to him, all he could think was they weren't Remington, which only made him madder.

He waited for all of them to gather around the table. They had a lot to go over and not a lot of time.

"Roam and Rascal, how's the tattoo shop going?"

"Good. Rascal and I have talked about getting security cameras at some point. There's no money missing but things have been off a couple times. Items misplaced. For a little while,

I thought I was just losing my mind because I was low on sleep because of the kids."

"Roam, it's not your imagination. I told you I thought I was just getting old. Things I know I put in my cabinet are suddenly in a different station or even in the office."

"Okay, Scoop's visiting his mom but when he gets back, have him look at a system. I think we need to upgrade all of them since we can't even keep the compound secure."

He paused. He knew Bear was going to chew them all out because he'd mentioned that gate multiple times. He agreed with Bear, but Baron and Rascal had pushed that they'd always had it that way. As the new president, he walked a fine line moving them forward while keeping the originals happy.

"If you all would have listened to me and taken care of it when I asked the previous hundreds of times, we wouldn't have had a problem."

"Nobody likes a know it all, Bear," Rascal sniped while glaring at his son.

"Okay, let's move on to the next item. We all know hindsight's twenty/twenty. We'll fix it."

It had taken him a couple of days after council to think of a suitable payback for the bike incident. Maybe if the pictures hadn't ended up all over, he could have let it slide but everywhere he went, someone mentioned it. Their Texas chapter had even sent a box of replacement supplies with pink heels with different decorations on them. Their note said his motorcycle wouldn't want to wear the same heels all the time.

He'd ridden to Dodge City today with Cannon to pick up some supplies for the gun shop. The guy at the gun shop made it a point to ask if all the Bluff Creek Brotherhood were redoing the bikes the same way. He'd grunted no, instead of hitting the guy like he wanted. He was proud he'd held back but it had been a trial. Cannon hadn't stopped laughing.

They'd stopped for lunch at a bar his dad recommended. He'd met the brothers Whiskey, Hennessey and Schaefer who owned the bar and had a lot to say about Remington and her sisters. The fact the girls were banned from the bar was nice because he now had one place he for sure could get away from Remington. Whiskey had been the one to inadvertently give him the idea for payback. He had no idea Remington still drove the 1976 metallic lime Chevy Monte Carlo the sisters had all learned how to drive in. He'd immediately texted Scoop on how to get access to the car. He appreciated classic cars just as much as he did motorcycles. He wouldn't hurt the car, just give Remington a little payback she deserved. He and Cannon could stop at the party store on the way out of town. His response would be appropriate to what she'd done to him, notifying her he wasn't a pushover, but it wouldn't be an escalation. At least, he didn't think it would be. Maybe he'd get a couple other opinions. He wasn't a fan of group texts, but is would probably be easiest for this.

War: Planning payback for Remington's crap with my bike. No escalating, just appropriate. Thinking glitter and confetti from the air vents and then decorations inside the Monte Carlo.

Bear: You sure you want to start this? Any reply is an escalation and women are devious.

Scoop: Seems pretty harmless to me. Annoying like yours was but not out of line. Even though she drives the car the most, the office has a duplicate set of keys on the wall. Easy enough to lift.

Flick: Glitter can cut or damage her eyes if it blows directly in her face. Confetti should be light enough you won't have to worry about hurting her.

Bear: Can we have warning and go into a partial lockdown? This is going to piss off your girl and I'd prefer to not be in the firing range.

War: She's not MY GIRL!

Cannon: I think he's protesting too much.

Roam: She's not going to see it as paying her back from your bike. She's going to see it as an escalation because the bike was payback for you calling her princess. Do what you want but don't come crying to me when it's an all-out war with all of her sisters. I've seen stuff over the years with how she handles a problem.

War: Are we an MC or is this preschool? She and her sisters aren't going to damage the relationship between us. Do we need to have some of you big babies go through prospecting again?

Scoop: I'm in.

Cannon: Ditto.

Bear: I never said I wasn't in, Mr. President. I asked if we could mitigate the retaliation which is what we do anytime we consider action against someone. Are your feelings a little touchy about her?

Baron: Retaliation is appropriate as long as Noah's car isn't damaged. I will not deal with the fallout from that.

War: Who the fuck added him to the text?

Rascal: I had Roam add us both because I was reading over his shoulder at the shop. You feel free to talk bad about us and let's see how your next tattoo looks.

War paused before replying. How had this gotten so out of control? His dad had a good point, but he wasn't in high school. He'd already considered how to do it without damaging the car. He had as much appreciation for the classic car as he did for his motorcycles, but it wasn't stopping him from a little payback. He'd gotten his responses and needed to shut this down.

War: I appreciate everyone's input. I'll get confetti instead of glitter. I want to inconvenience not hurt anyone.

He and Cannon needed to get on the road and get back. It wasn't that he didn't appreciate Baron and Rascal's input. It was having someone else make the decision for him. Roam still deferred to his dad, which he could understand because Baron had been president a long time, but Roam needed to stop seeing his dad in that capacity and accept him as president.

Chapter Eight

Remington walked out her door, sliding on her sunglasses. She and Winnie were going to take the Monte Carlo to Dodge City for a little retail therapy. She'd texted to see if anyone else wanted to go with them, but they'd all been busy. The plus of going with just Winnie was they dressed alike so they wouldn't hit any of the shops that only sold dresses.

She stopped and knocked on Winnie's door before going in. They all had an open-door policy but knocked first. Winnie didn't care about knocking but Remington did. She wanted to know if her door flew open without a knock, it was an indication the one coming in might not be a friendly.

"I'll be right out!" Winnie yelled.

How did she know Winnie wouldn't be quite ready? Winnie was punctual with anything work related but in her personal life, she was a free spirit. Well, at least concerning time. When they'd lost their mom to breast cancer, Winnie had turned into a health nut. Deep down she was sure Winnie knew their mom eating healthy wouldn't have changed the outcome, but it was Winnie's way of having a semblance of control over the uncontrollable.

"Okay, I'm ready." Winnie breezed out of the bedroom in tight, ripped jeans, motorcycle boots and a navy-blue tank top. Her only jewelry was her watch. Winnie was fanatical about getting her exercise and steps in. Grabbing a crossbody leather bag, Winnie arched her eyebrow impatiently at Remington then immediately walked out the door.

"Thanks for coming with me. I needed a break."

"No problem. I'm always up for shopping and spending time with my sisters. Is it just us this time? I gave up on the group text when it went off like fifty times."

"Yep. Everybody was busy but they all requested we stop by the new bakery on the way back and buy treats." Remington smiled as she unlocked the car. She was glad it had been parked in the shade by the garage. She didn't need her hands burning from the metallic steering wheel. "Do you know where you want to go first?"

She slid in, putting the key in the ignition while rolling down the windows. As hot as it was, she wanted some breeze before she turned on the air conditioner. Although the A/C was good in the car, it took a little bit to get where she needed it in the Kansas heat. Whoever had driven it last hadn't put up the sunshade. She'd be leaving a note by the keys in the office. It wasn't like it was rocket science to leave the car how you found it.

"I'm thinking the leather shop. I'd like to look at another jacket and maybe boots. Will you turn on the A/C? I know you have this whole routine but I'm melting."

"Hold your horses. You know Ginger responds better if she warms up a little first."

Remington slid the seat a little closer. Her dad must have driven it last because she rarely needed to slide it closer. She clipped her seatbelt, waited another minute, then turned the A/C to high before flipping it on.

"Cold air for the..." Remington coughed as flecks of something covered her and got in her mouth. She spit, wiping her mouth and face, trying to see what had happened. Winnie's laughter clued her in something was going on.

She shook her hair, then wiped whatever was over her eyes off so she could see. Looking down, she saw pink pieces of paper. At first, she thought it was confetti but then she realized it was hole punches and they were everywhere. She looked a little closer. Did the freaking hole punches have crowns on them? Oh no he didn't. She glanced in the mirror and saw the air conditioner had blown it all in her hair and on her shirt.

"Looks like War didn't appreciate what you did to his bike." Winnie's gleeful voice had her seriously considering shoving her out of the car. Of course, it looked like Winnie's air vents hadn't been messed with. War wasn't willing to just take his punishment like a good boy and had decided to retaliate. Now that she was over the shock, she could appreciate his prank. As long as he hadn't hurt Ginger and sent the paper through her air intake, then she'd consider them even. If he'd hurt her baby, he'd have more than her to deal with. Her dad still washed the car weekly and took her on a drive down Main Street each week. He also alternated taking her to his Saturday coffee and cruising group. Heck, if War had done something to the air intake, she would make sure she was far away from her dad when he found out. Her dad was fair, but he'd been a member of the MC for years and head of their bail bonds company. He didn't take any crap from anyone, and Ginger was special to him. It's the car they all learned to drive in but more than that, it was the one her mom drove until the day she died.

"So, are we driving Ginger, or do we need to get her checked out first?"

"Let's take another car. I think War would be smart enough to not send the stuff through the intake vents but I'm not taking any chances. We'll let Jesse check her out."

Winnie jumped out and ran toward her Jeep. "Dibs on driving!"

Crap. She'd fallen right into that. Now she had to deal with her speed demon sister all the way to Dodge City. She owed War for that, too, and she'd be paying him back. He had no idea what he'd started. He should have just taken her advice and quit calling her princess. She turned the car off and grabbed the sunshade from the back. At least when Jesse came to get Ginger, the steering wheel wouldn't burn her hands. She flipped the visor down to secure the sunshade then got out of the car.

Winnie pulled her Jeep up then started laughing. "Oh, Remi, he's got your number."

She glanced where Winnie was pointing. Her sunshade for Ginger had been decorated with pictures of crowns and pink heels but honestly, the part that irritated her the most was his words. How did the man know exactly what to say to get her boiling mad?

Princess Remington,

Everybody knows a princess can't ever get one over on the king.

King War

So, he was a king, and she was a princess? It was a good thing they were going shopping out of town, so she'd have some time to calm down. Maybe her decorating his bike hadn't been her smartest move for a good business relationship but he was the one to choose to bring childhood nicknames into their business.

She wasn't sure why his opinion of her mattered so much, but she couldn't seem to let it go. Maybe chatting with Winnie and shopping could help her get her head on straight. She really wanted to talk with Regina because after they'd lost their mom, Regina had been her sounding board. Regina would love nothing more than to see them married with kids on the way. She was the exact person Remi couldn't talk to about this.

Times like this she really missed her mom. Her mom had been tough but had always had a hug and the right words to help them get to the heart of the problem. It had been ten years and she still sometimes forgot and picked up the phone to ask her a question.

Crying over spilt milk, or in this case blown confetti, wouldn't help the problem. She and Winnie would get some shopping in and maybe chat about her fascination with the man who made her blood boil.

Chapter Nine

War walked into the building, cataloguing exits and any threats. His dad had informed the MC that it was the quarterly fight nights at the training academy. He instructed them to have clothes to change into just in case they were needed for demonstrations or possibly a match. When he questioned Matt, who he still had a hard time remembering to call Roam, he'd acted like it was a normal part of fight nights. He wasn't sure why Roam's road name was harder to remember than others but maybe it was because he'd been his brother Matty forever and then Matt in high school and then he'd had a nickname in the military.

Roam was struggling with being a single parent even with all the brothers' help but there seemed to be something more. His outlook on life was the polar opposite from when they'd talked on the phone. He'd thought he'd understood what being president entailed but he had been missing a huge part. He wasn't a touchy, feely type of guy but it seemed like he'd need to work on that. Keeping the brotherhood together was more than meeting once a week and talking about businesses. He only hoped he could live up to his dad's legacy.

Winnie jumped up on the elevated ring closest to the door, grabbing a microphone. She tapped the microphone twice to get everyone's attention. She was the middle sister and gorgeous by his standards, but she did nothing for him. It was the tall brunette in the tank top and shorts who had his interest. Her hair was in an intricate braid, which was twirled low at the back of her head. She was standing by a group of girls who he'd guess were high school or college age.

"Welcome to exhibition night at the academy. Tonight, we have a couple of special additions. We have four students who have passed their gold level and will be sparring tonight, so let's get started."

Two high school age boys with boxing gear on made their way into the ring. Beth had a t-shirt with the gym's name on it and referee in print. She had them tap gloves then walk back five steps, then blew the whistle. The boys did some footwork around each other. He idly watched to see who would take the first punch. The one boy must have been watching. His opponent telegraphed with his body language what he was going to do but the watcher struck first, landing a hard blow to his head. From then, it was constant action for the rest of the round. The boys were evenly matched and enjoyable to watch. Whoever had taught them had done a good job.

Beth blew the whistle at the end of the round and the boys retreated to their corners. A man he didn't know was talking with one boy and Winnie was talking with the watcher. She turned and demonstrated something to him, patted his shoulder and smiled. The kid nodded his head.

He'd had no idea Franks and Daughters Bail Bonds had multiple businesses. Bail bonds was a lot, but it seemed like they'd diversified.

A shoulder bump heralded Roam beside him.

"Pretty impressive, huh?"

"Yeah, it is. It seems lucrative, too."

Roam nodded. "I know it is, but the students tonight are all scholarship ones, I believe."

"Scholarship?"

"Beth is the youngest, but that woman can squeeze money from a turnip. She visits different businesses and asks for their support. Adults, unless they're coming through Remington's contacts, pay to learn self-defense, boxing and other disciplines. Anyone in school is offered a scholarship if the sisters have any inkling that they can't pay. Scholarship students, though, are required to help out and volunteer their time for the younger kids."

He ached to ask what Roam meant about Remington's contacts but his quieter voice when he mentioned it told him all he needed to know. He'd ask about it when they were in a secure place without all the unwanted ears around. The building was impressive. He'd guessed it was one of the larger metal barn structures but inside, you'd never tell the sides were metal. Sheetrocked walls and ceilings had it looking like a high-end gym. Mirrors were interspersed on the walls beside weights where people could check their form. Positive sayings were painted on different parts of the wall. A couple places had levels written and names were signed underneath.

Besides designated restrooms, there were locker rooms at one end of the structure. The outside had looked a little strange to him when he walked up. Instead of seeing metal in a solid color, there were designs on the outside of the building. It had been getting dark enough he couldn't tell if it had been done with wood or paint. Everything about this and the event made him curious to know more about Remington. It would help if she looked at him with something other than disdain.

Thinking about her had him missing the other boys' exhibition and both of the girls' matches. It was a good thing he was in a safe location because if he'd been in danger, someone would have gotten the drop on him. He wasn't usually this distracted. Winnie hopped back in the ring with a huge smile on her face. Why did he get the feeling he wasn't going to like what she said? It might have had something to do with the clothes his dad had directed them all to bring.

"Are you all ready for our next treat tonight? Our local MC has graciously offered up some men to help a couple of our instructors demonstrate what you can achieve no matter your size. We'll give War, Bear and Remington a little time to make sure they are in comfortable clothes. I'll be joining in on this, too. We'll take a ten-minute break, so everyone grab some snacks."

He glanced over at his mom and dad as he walked with his clothes toward the locker room. His mom's smirk indicated this might be payback for lunch awhile back. He'd apologized but it seemed like he had some more penance. He wasn't sure why Bear was getting penalized but at least it wasn't just him.

"I get why I'm doing this but what did you do to warrant this?"

Bear walked ahead, kicking off his shoes and opening a locker to hang his cut in.

"I volunteered. Winnie and Beth suggested using guys who hadn't helped in any of the training because it would be a good demonstration. I knew after last week you would be the other one and I got bonus points for volunteering."

Sometimes he wondered why he considered Bear his best friend when he hadn't had his back in this instance but knowing his mom, she'd threatened to bar Bear from her kitchen if he said a word. Since they'd gotten back, Bear was in there a lot helping his mom. During one of their stakeouts with way too much coffee, he'd admitted that when his dad had gotten custody of him and brought him to the MC, he hadn't believed moms acted like Regina. He'd fallen in love with cooking with her and baking. It was the first time he'd felt like he had a home. War had been too young when Bear came to them to understand what had happened but over the years, he'd pieced together his friend had a lot of trauma from childhood packed away.

He opened the locker with his name on it, shrugging out of his cut and hanging it up. He pulled out a bag labeled 'wear this' and opened it. A jock strap with a cup was inside. He'd brought his own jockstrap and in boxing, he wouldn't need a cup. He shoved it back in the locker and yanked off his t-shirt. He'd go out there and do his best. Hopefully, being a good sport would get him back in his mom's good graces. Remington had played her prank and he'd retaliated. They were even and he was going to work toward getting along with her and remind himself to not call her princess. He'd called her that in his head for years and breaking the habit was going to be hard. For the good of his MC, he didn't see any option but treating Remington a little nicer, which included not needling her, at least not where anyone else could hear. Bear was scheduled on a protection detail with them this week, but he was scheduled for one three weeks away.

Following Bear back out to the ring, he reminded himself he needed to be careful. He didn't know their skills and wouldn't want to embarrass them in front of their students. He'd be cautious until he assessed their level.

Winnie was back up in the ring with Remington but this time, Remington was holding the mic.

"Looks like we're ready to start. Winnie and Bear are going to start us off with a little boxing. They have not been opponents before so they'll both have to assess skills. Any guesses on who will come out on top?"

"The guy, of course!" one of the high school guys yelled out.

"Interesting. Bear does have some muscle mass and knows how to fight. Anyone else?"

"Winchester's going to kick his butt, Ms. Franks. He's not going to know what hit him," one of the girls commented.

"Winnie does have a few skills which could help her in this. We'll do a two-minute match. I particularly want you all to watch and dissect why they are choosing to use the punches they use."

Bear and Winnie touched gloves and a man with a referee shirt blew a whistle to start the match. Bear hung back, waiting on Winnie. She did some good footwork as she moved around Bear. He couldn't quite hear what she was saying but he could see Bear's face scowling. Quicker than he'd thought she faked a right hook then followed up with her left, which Bear didn't see coming. He was sure if Bear didn't have the protective helmet on and her hands weren't in gloves, he'd be out on the floor. The power behind her jab surprised him.

Bear and she traded punches but were evenly matched. The referee blew the whistle, and the judges declared a tie.

Beth hopped up into the ring, grinning. "It looks to me that you can't tell who will be the winner by size or the sex of the opponents. It all comes down to skill. Our next volunteers are going to demonstrate some self-defense. War is going to try to take Remington down to the mat by any means necessary and pin her for ten seconds. Remington's job is to not allow that. We're going to let War decide if he wants to approach from the front or the back and we'll set a two-minute time limit."

Beth motioned him and Remington up. He knew Remington had some skills because they recovered fugitives and she was tall, so he didn't have much of a height advantage. He'd take any advantage, so he'd approach from behind.

Remington was ready for War. To be honest, she'd been looking forward to this way too much. Even if they ended up as a tie, she wanted a chance to teach him a lesson. She wasn't particularly bloodthirsty but something about his attitude scraped on her last nerve.

She'd helped grow the business even when it required getting down and dirty, but he still saw her with a warped sense of who she was. She wasn't even sure why his opinion mattered but it did. She usually had thick skin. In her job, you had to. So many men and women called her names because she was in a male-dominated profession. She brushed it off and forgot it but with War, there wasn't any brushing it away. She couldn't sleep last night thinking about tonight. How she wanted him to truly see her for the woman she was, not the girl he imagined.

She'd known he'd go for the approach from behind. His ego was large, but he was smart, too, and would use any advantage he could. She'd coerced one of the employees from the security business who was similar in size and weight to War into practicing with her yesterday. He was why she'd included the cup in War's locker. She hadn't been trying to hit him in the crotch, but she'd landed a high thigh kick and almost had her employee crying on the mats. He'd said it was his own fault for not wearing the right equipment, but she'd still bought him supper and a six-pack of beer as an apology.

Bear caught her attention at the side of the ring as he flicked on the sound system and Pat Benatar's "Hit Me With Your Best Shot" filled the arena. After having a tie with Winnie, Bear was probably hoping for his brother to take her down. He was, first and foremost, War's brother in the MC and bragging rights were a huge deal.

She centered herself as War walked behind her. Blocking out the sound of the crowd and the music, she listened for him. He was too big of a man to be silent even on the softened ring floor. His footsteps, although quiet, were noticeable. They quickened and she prepared. She'd love to turn around and meet him head on, but she wasn't bending the rules. When she won or tied, it would be because of her skill. No matter how much she wanted to win, she also wanted to demonstrate to the students that size could be overcome by skill and knowledge—at least most of the time.

His arms wrapped around her biceps, pinning her arms to her chest. She only had seconds before he would try to force her to the mats. She picked her feet up and let him absorb all her weight. He wasn't quite prepared for it, and she slipped down farther in his arms. With all but her shoulders free, she rammed her head back, hitting his chin as she drove her clasped fists up, knocking one of his arms away.

He grappled to take control, holding on to her left arm as she dropped to one knee. She grasped his upper arm, using it for balance. She turned until she was perpendicular with him and kicked out with her left leg, using his hold for balance. Her foot connected with his inside thigh near his groin and slid hard into his crotch, only she didn't hit the plastic of his cup, she connected with soft tissue. His hold loosened as he clasped his crotch and dropped to his knees. He groaned, gasping for breath.

She leaned toward him, putting her hand on his shoulder to check him and he tilted away as if he was worried she'd hit him again.

"War, I'm not trying to hit you. Are you okay? I am so sorry."

He shook his head as Winnie and Bear joined them. A retching sound came from his throat.

"Do you need help out of the ring?" Bear offered a hand up.

Each second he didn't answer made her feel horrible. She'd wanted to teach him a lesson but not actually hurt him. Why the heck didn't he wear the cup she'd left for him?

Nothing was going as she planned. Her only goal tonight was to teach the kids and have him see her for the woman she was—strong, capable and the complete opposite of a princess.

WAR

War concentrated on breathing, fighting the waves of nausea. The pain from her kick had him wanting to curl up on the mat. The fact he was still on his knees was a win in his book. He choked, trying to keep from puking on the mats. A hand touched his shoulder and he leaned away—he was seconds from losing it and he needed to keep control.

He was fucking thankful it hadn't been a direct hit. At least it was only a glancing blow and she'd hit his thigh first. It was probably the only thing keeping him from being seriously hurt.

She'd apologized but he couldn't worry about making her feel better. The pain stopping or at least receding a little was crucial before he could move. He ignored Bear's voice offering to help him out of the ring because there was no way he could move. He was seconds from tears so moving wasn't happening.

"Hey, War, I've got an ice pack," Flick stated as he pulled War's hand away and placed the ice pack against him. It was so cold but a welcome distraction. He swallowed and breathed deep, praying the nausea would go away. At least with Flick, he had an EMT taking care of him. He couldn't imagine having to go to the hospital about this. Nope, not happening. He'd limp out of the ring in just a second when he could breathe. The tears welled again at the thought of having to ride his motorcycle along the bumpy road.

"Let's give that a minute to work, then we'll move him out of the ring."

"I feel horrible. I never would have tried a thigh kick if I'd known he didn't wear the cup."

His pain even overshadowed hearing the misery in Remington's voice. She shouldn't feel guilty. It was his fault for being cocky. He couldn't let her feel bad, though. He'd tell her as soon as he could form words. The pain was receding a little with the ice.

"Here." Flick's hand holding out pain pills had him opening his mouth and letting him hold the water bottle while he washed it down. He wasn't moving his hands until he was positive it wouldn't send him crying to the mat.

He vaguely heard Winnie explaining what had happened and how they could learn from this. He was sure he'd see this as a learning experience later, when he didn't want to curl in a ball. He took a couple deeper breaths, blowing out slowly. He wasn't sure how long he'd been sitting here but he could open his eyes and leave them open without wanting to puke.

He looked up at Remington's worried face. She didn't look like a princess. She looked like a badass female who had knocked him on his ass.

"Not your fault. Quit worrying," he whispered, testing his voice to make sure he wouldn't cry.

At the sound of his voice, Flick and Bear grabbed an arm. "Let's get you up and out of here. We're going to take one of the Franks' SUVs. Remington can ride your bike then bring the SUV back."

He nodded. He assumed if she was offering to ride his bike, she had enough experience and at this point, he just wanted out of the ring and to lie down somewhere.

Remington caught the keys Winnie tossed to her. Winnie followed with the rest of their stuff as Bear and Flick finally tired of waiting for War to try to walk. Wrapping his arms around their shoulders, they lifted him off his feet and walked to the waiting SUV.

Her stomach ached. Between worrying about War and the guilt of what she'd done, however unintentional, she was glad to have to ride to get away for a little bit. His voice croaking out it wasn't her fault was nice, but she'd hurt him.

She changed into her jeans, riding boots and a shirt with a little more coverage, grabbing her leather jacket, too. Firing up War's motorcycle, she listened to the comforting growl. Since she was little, the growl of a motorcycle had always meant safety and love. Her mom had only ridden on the back of her dad's bike. She'd never had her own. Remington had anticipated when it was her turn on the back of her dad's bike but always knew she wanted her own. Before War had crushed her adolescent dreams, she'd imagined them on long rides and picnics together under the stars.

Even after their relationship had turned, he'd still appeared in her fantasies and dreams periodically. He was her perfect man in almost every way. She admired his strength of character and his protective nature. He'd grown up with a mom and dad who were all about family. His commitment to his family and brothers would make him a great father and oh my, she'd always been drawn in by his eyes. A deep, dark brown which reminded her of toffee—decadent, sweet pools of toffee she could fall into if she let herself. They twinkled with a glint when he laughed, which around his family was a given.

He topped her by about four inches which was saying something since she was six foot tall in her stocking feet. She'd actually be able to lay her head on his shoulder. He had muscles accented by his tattoos. He was lickable and she was so freaking ready to take a swipe and taste him.

But then, he'd call her princess and she'd be ready to either slap some sense into him or shoot his feet with her gun, making him dance until he changed his tune.

She followed the SUV, but she didn't need to. She could make this drive in her sleep. The gate to the compound opened as the SUV approached. One of the guys must have called ahead so they wouldn't need a code because no one got in after dark without stopping.

Regina had been pushing the guys to add openers in all the vehicles but Bear had vehemently opposed, and the brothers agreed. He'd gone into this long, drawn out scenario with the gist of it being what if their enemies got ahold of an opener? They could be attacked unaware.

She loved his worst-case scenarios mentality. He'd still been working for the police department when they built the gym, but she'd consulted with him over email about safety precautions. The building hid a couple surprises she prayed they'd never have to use but if they were needed, they'd be prepared. He'd also consulted on a couple of other projects. His brain was a treasure trove of ideas even if his demeanor was off-putting to most.

WAR

She backed War's bike into the president's spot beside the clubhouse. The guys had disappeared with War into the clubhouse, most likely to his room. Not that she'd been nosy and asked where War was staying.

Roam was still staying at his parents' house with the little ones, and she could see War wanting the comradery of the clubhouse but also a place without little ones crying. Unless she'd missed some gossip, he'd always lived alone after he got out of the Army. And despite the way they'd parted, she'd always kept an ear out for any news about him. Even as angry as she'd been when he'd left, she'd prayed every day for the safety of them while they served.

For a Saturday night, it was exceptionally quiet. Most of the guys had been over at the gym or some of them were on a security job. She followed the voices back to War's room.

"Thanks for getting me here but I don't fucking need your help getting my jeans off. We'll just leave them on until tomorrow."

She bit her lip, hiding a grin.

"I get it. The last thing you want is to have us tug and pull your jeans off, but I am an EMT. You are either letting me check you, or Bear and I will drag your sorry ass back out to the SUV and take you to the emergency room."

She paused in the doorway with the keys. War's eyes widened at her appearance. She wasn't staying for the unveiling but not because she didn't want to. Oh, she'd love to get a glimpse of his package but only if and when he wanted her to.

"Sorry to interrupt. Here's the bike key and I'm so sorry, War. I never meant to hurt you."

Laying the bike key on his dresser, she turned to leave but stopped at his words.

"I know you didn't. Thanks for bringing my bike and don't think there won't be a rematch. I'll just make sure next time I wear all provided safety equipment."

His smile was more of a grimace. He was still in a lot of pain.

"Thanks, War. I'll leave so you can get some rest."

Heading out, she listened to War giving in and then groaning as they removed his jeans. He'd be okay. If Flick was seriously worried, they would have never brought him to the clubhouse first. He would have taken him to the closest ER, which wasn't close at all, approximately forty miles. It was why she and her dad had been discussing adding in a small clinic and partnering with the brotherhood. With Flick's expertise and a couple others, it would be nice to not have to drive for care, especially if it wasn't a major emergency.

Seeing War helped her a little, but she'd figure out some other way to show she was sorry, unless as soon as he wasn't in pain, he turned back into the guy that called her princess. Then, all bets would be off.

Chapter Ten

Remington glanced at the schedule. Bear and Winchester had been partnered on a security gig last week and done well. The client had even included a tip because he'd appreciated their thoroughness. She bet they'd been thorough. Mr. and Mrs. Worst-Case Scenario would have talked through the million and one ways something could go wrong. He'd been a high-profile client and she'd known they'd work well together. Winnie had been a little irritable because she'd wanted to work with Bear and had argued with her until she'd finally agreed.

She was completely ignoring next week because she and War were scheduled for a security detail, an overnight. In fact, she needed to schedule him at the range with her this week. Her policy required that all new security detail officers had to go to the range with her. He'd been a police officer and she was positive he could shoot but there were details you picked up watching someone shoot on the range and then run the tactical course. Details that could be the edge they needed if things went from sugar to shit, which could happen no matter how much planning she did.

After her apology, she'd mistakenly assumed lunch at the clubhouse would be enjoyable and War would be civil. Whether it was because he was in pain or because he was being an ass, she'd bided her time and hadn't really enjoyed her lunch with all the little digs he'd made. When she'd thanked Regina for the meal but said she had a prior engagement, Roam had touched her arm and mouthed 'sorry.' Why he thought he needed to apologize for his jerk of a brother, she wasn't sure.

Frankly, his attitude was strange with the changes. Maybe she'd have Sarah do a deep dive into his background. Because he was a member of the MC and had been around the family forever, they'd foregone the major background checks they normally did.

Possibly she was missing something, and she despised feeling like she didn't have all the pieces to the puzzle. After she got back from the range, she'd schedule Sarah to dig deeper but if she didn't leave now, she'd be late.

She grabbed the keys and walked out of the office. "Heading to the range."

Winnie hopped up from behind her desk. "I'm going with."

She paused and stared. Why would Winnie go? She'd just been there yesterday picking up a new gun and spending time on the range getting familiar with it. She cocked her eyebrow waiting for Winnie to explain. They'd done this so many times that who knew which one of them would win the standoff.

Winnie finally huffed and shook her head. "You are so maddening. Can't I just go to the range with my sister?"

"Maybe if you hadn't been in a while. What gives?"

"I heard Bear say he was going to watch you two and I want to also."

Are you freaking kidding me? Like she needed any of the peanut gallery watching them, especially when she had no idea which War she'd end up with. The sweet one who said she didn't need to be sorry or the ass who was still calling her princess. Unless princesses wore motorcycle boots, he'd need to find another name to call her.

"Fine. You can keep me from killing War if he annoys me."

"Oh. Maybe we need backup if you're considering that." Winnie tapped on her phone and then slid it back in her pocket.

"What did you do?"

"Code Rachel."

She loved her sisters and she needed to remind herself of that because what Winnie had just done had her ready to be an only child. Now, they'd all be up in her business on the course and depending on if her sisters were with other employees when they got the text, she might have more backup than she wanted. Some days it didn't pay to get up and get out of bed, and today might be one of those days.

Her plans were to have her and War run the outdoor course and the indoor course separately while the other person watched. She'd given him a couple weeks to heal. Not to pinpoint any errors but to get a feel how their partner acted in any situation. She and Bear had done the same thing before she added him as her partner on security. A couple of their employees had grumbled about having to run it with each of the sisters before their first time on a detail or skip together. She'd sent them packing.

Their jobs required them to stay in shape. Even if they weren't running through the course because of a new partner, Franks and Daughters Bail Bonds employees were required to put in time, staying in shape and keeping sharp on their firearms. Each employee, besides going through a rigorous vetting process, also had to make it past each sister in the interviews. They each had different traits they were looking for. If anyone didn't meet a standard by one of the sisters, they were immediately dropped.

Having a rigorous process had cut down on their turnover. She was proud of what they'd built even though some days she dreamed of having a family and taking care of them. She wouldn't quit her job for her family, but their business had the flexibility of doing both. They'd all met and discussed how they'd handle children when they found their one, their soulmate, and decided to have a family. Sarah and Beth had put together a plan to bump out the house, moving the tech to the outside wall and add an on-site daycare. Because Sarah believed in planning ahead, the foundation was laid and workers were starting even though none of them were dating anyone serious.

She wanted someone serious but not just anyone would do. She and her sisters wouldn't settle for anything less than what their parents had—their other half, the person they couldn't imagine living without. Call her corny or living in a fairy tale but she wasn't giving up on having her dream even though sometimes it was hard to keep the faith. Holding Roam's twins and snuggling them with their baby smell brought home what she didn't have. She even considered doing IVF, but she wanted to share a baby with the man she loved, nothing less would do for her. She still had a little time.

War was waiting at the counter of the tactical training portion of the gun store. He honestly looked better every time she saw him, which was maddening. If she had a clue which personality she'd get today, she could prepare. She wanted the one back who was kind and told her it wasn't her fault. Maybe kicking him in the crotch again would get her the personality she liked best, but it definitely wasn't a long-term solution.

"You're going to be so glad you scheduled this today, Remington. I have something special for you to look at after you're done with the course. I don't want to show you now because your drooling might affect your time on the course," Cannon called out as she approached the desk.

He was going to make her jealous. She just knew it. They'd been discussing their favorite guns and ones on their wish lists. She sure as heck hoped he had something for her to buy and not something he bought only for himself. She'd rejoice with him over his new gun, but he'd been looking for a special one for her.

"Should I have brought my wallet?"

His grin as he shook his head had her wishing she found him attractive. He seemed easygoing but no, she had to pant after the big guy next to him with the frown on his face. Guess it was testy War she was stuck with today. She much preferred tantalizing War with his sweet mouth and his dreamy eyes.

"I'm not telling. Good girls have to earn the privilege."

Holy hotness. Those words from his mouth would have Jesse drooling if she was here. She was constantly reading the romance novels with a dominant man and wanted to find one in real life. Not that Remi didn't read those romance novels, too. She did. She wanted a strong man but one who saw her as a partner. Too dominant and he'd piss her off.

"Okay. Let's get started. I'll run tactical one while you watch from above and then you'll run tactical two while I watch. It's not a competition on how fast you run it. It's for us to learn how the other reacts to situations so we can be a more effective team. Then we'll do some practice at the shooting range while the scenarios are reset, and we'll run the other ones. Any questions?"

"I don't think so. I'm looking forward to working with you."

Now, she was freaking confused. His attitude when she'd walked in and his demeanor had led her to believe she was going to be getting testy War. His tone and words didn't match. She'd get through this. He was home for good, and she didn't have choice. She had to figure out how they could work together.

War scrutinized everything about Remington as she went through the course. Her form and response time were solid and would have put her at the top of any class at the academy.

The next target popped up. He shook his head. Cannon or whoever set up the course had put War's picture on the face of the enemy target. Remington paused for a split second, thrown by the image, then shot his picture in the head, missing the child held in the target's arms. He understood why they'd done it, but he didn't have to agree with his brothers. Remington and he were going to be protecting a client and needed to be ready for anything. He only hoped Remington didn't think he'd done it as a joke. He'd promised himself he was going to treat her as a colleague today, including asking her to lunch to get to know her better.

He'd been an ass again at Sunday lunch. He'd still been hurting a little, but he'd also been embarrassed by the whole incident. He hadn't responded well and had taken out his temper by sniping at Remington. If he could figure out what was triggering his response, maybe he could change it. He had been hurting but honestly, the reason he'd been sniping at her was he felt like an outsider. He was the president of Bluff Creek Brotherhood MC, yet he was constantly being hit in the face with all the things no one told him. He hadn't been around much over the years so he could see his dad spending the time celebrating and not with business, but he'd been home for three months. Surely someone could have taken the time to update him on *his* MC.

Maybe Remington could help him out and, in the process, he could make amends enough to appease his mom along with smoothing over their working relationship. He had no doubt she'd enjoy schooling him on all the things he'd missed out on. She'd irritated him when they were younger because he'd thought she was a little miss know-it-all. He was wondering if his view had been skewed. From what Roam had said, she'd hit every goal she'd ever set and was so freaking smart. He wasn't sold on her being perfect but maybe he'd reacted and judged her without getting to know the adult Remington. She was gorgeous and having her appear in his dreams last night didn't help, but he'd ignored his urges before. It wouldn't be the first time. Bear nudged him.

"She's solid and great on security. You don't have any worries."

Being thirty feet above the tactical course and plexiglass in between them and the course meant they weren't required to wear ear protection or glasses. If he had on the ear protection, he'd have an excuse for not hearing his best friend. Bear and he had worked in the same divisions but hadn't been partnered until about six years ago. He wasn't sure he could have continued if he hadn't known he could trust the partner at his back. He'd almost quit then, but he'd still been sure he could help people. Their chief had proved him wrong. He'd known it was time to come home.

He nodded to indicate he'd heard but he wasn't discussing any more with all the ears listening right now. He wasn't airing his dirty laundry and it wouldn't affect his performance on the security job. Remington cleared the course and looked at her score. She kicked the edge of the board walking toward the exit. She'd had a phenomenal time and record. Why was she unhappy with her stats?

"Rem was a little slower with that switch up in the course. Was that your idea?" Winnie's glare at him would've had a lesser man shriveling but he held his ground.

"It wasn't me."

"Cannon and I decided it was a good idea to switch up some of the course pop-ups. We do this course weekly. While the placement of the targets changes, the actual faces haven't been changed since we opened. Getting stale could have ramifications. We can't compromise the safety of our clients or the members of our team."

Jesse had an excellent point. War nodded then headed down the stairs for his turn. He kept his eyes off the course as it was reset. No way was he giving Remington any ammunition for teasing him that he was cheating. If he was going to beat her, and he was going to try his hardest, he'd win fairly.

Remington was waiting for him inside the locker room.

"Good run."

"Yeah, they got me having that picture of you, but I understand. Here's your gun and your course safety gear. You'll go out this door, holding at the yellow line. The light will change from red to green along with a loud buzz when your turn starts. There should be about twenty targets that pop up as you make your way through the course. There are a couple of choices as you go through. Some have more targets. Some have less."

"Got it. Thanks." He watched her leave, admiring how her tactical pants highlighted the curve of her ass, knowing he didn't have time to admire her ass when he was here to practice for their security detail. *Fucking focus, War.*

He hadn't run a course since they'd been home and he'd been so focused on his case before he left the department, it had probably been a year since he'd run one. He'd kept up on his range time, but he'd been slacking. Time to see how he stacked up to Remington.

Remington smiled at her sisters and the guys exchanging money. She and War had finished with a tie between the two competitions. Bear was the one winning all the bets and was actually sporting a small grin. It had done what she needed. War had seen her skills and she'd analyzed his. She was confident they could work together on the detail in two weeks.

Cannon had said she'd been a good girl doing the course even with the changes and shown her his purchase but said he could order a second if she was interested. The Beretta 80X Cheetah was a beauty with the bronze grip and the optics slide was perfect. She told him to hold off on ordering it. She'd bought a new gun three weeks ago and should wait for any new toys.

She was starving and some of the time they all met for lunch but right now, she needed a break from her sisters. Maybe she could heat up leftovers at the house, although today the diner had meatloaf on the menu. He only offered it once a week and it was one of her favorites.

"Hey, I feel like I got us off on the wrong foot. Besides hurting, I've been a little put out about all the things I didn't know. I'd like to take you to lunch and apologize. Maybe you could help me out by giving me a rundown of some of the major changes."

She'd steeled herself to be around him for the hours on the course and now, he was wanting to extend it. His hopeful tone seemed at odds with the War she'd been encountering lately. It was the absolute last thing she wanted to do but they would be working together soon. Maybe she should. Maybe being around him would help her to not focus on how his full lips looked nestled in his beard and how they'd feel against her. Seeing his tattoos across the table from her might help her quit imagining tracing them with her tongue. Maybe she just needed to be exposed to him a little more and his attitude would turn her attention from everything she thought about him at night.

"Okay."

The look of surprise on his face most likely matched hers because she'd answered before she even realized what she was doing.

"Do you want to ride on my bike?"

At that, she smirked. She'd taken her bike today for their competition because it was one of the few sunny days this week and she'd needed the calming drive to prepare for today.

"Thanks, but mine's out front. It will be easier to follow you then leave directly from there for my next appointment. I don't want to have to backtrack to here."

She put her helmet on, fastening it, then started up her baby, a 2009 Harley Davidson Softail Deluxe, and followed behind War out onto the road leading to the highway. She appreciated he wasn't taking the back way. It had been dry and with the road being dirt, she would have been coated in the fine red dust. If she didn't know War better, she'd think he was disappointed she wasn't riding with him, but he wouldn't care. He was making nice with her because they would be working together. Plus, she was positive Regina had probably had a little chat with him after last Sunday's lunch. Sunday was the only time Regina demanded all the MC be there for lunch. They were her family whether by blood or choice and she used the time to check on them.

When her mom was alive, their family would join the MC at least once a month for Sunday lunch. After they'd lost her mom, Regina had been the one helping her hold the family together. They'd all been adults when they lost her, but her dad had gone into a deep depression. Regina had worried about all of them and made the rule they would all be at Sunday lunch unless they were sick or gone on a job. It had been one of the best things for them. It gave Regina a chance to check on each of them and help them through the grief process. Baron and Rascal had taken it upon themselves to be there for her dad.

She backed into the parking space that the diner kept out front for motorcycles. He had six spaces specifically for motorcycles. As a biker himself, he wanted them to know they were always welcome. His diner had been around back when the MC formed in 1977. Some of the townspeople hadn't been quite as thrilled but most had come around when they saw all the good the MC did and the protection they provided as a courtesy to their neighbors. He and Regina had been partners in the early years, but he'd bought out her share when Regina had decided it was too much when she was pregnant with her and Baron's fourth child.

She followed War up to the diner door where he held it open for her. When was the last time a man opened the door for her? Sure, she could open it herself and she wanted to be seen as strong when she was working but if she went out on a date, she wanted the guy to treat her a little special. Today wasn't a date but War's holding the door was nice.

She waved at the owner as she grabbed her favorite booth. One side allowed you to see the front door and the other allowed you to see the door from the hallway which led to the back parking lot. When a couple of the other businesses on the street complained about the diner taking all the parking, the owner had bought the lot behind him and turned it into a parking lot. On Saturdays, rain or shine, he allowed the townspeople to set up booths to sell their items whether it was food, crafts or thrift. He had a whole system set up to give everyone a chance. She loved how he gave back to the community. War gave her a questioning glance when she allowed him to choose which side he'd rather have.

She slid into the seat and leaned forward, whispering, "I'll tell you my secret if you promise you won't share. I don't want my favorite booth always taken." At his nod, she continued. "Your side obviously can see the front door. About five years ago, he added a back parking lot and a door in the hallway to it. This booth is perfect because either side gives you at least one of the entrances and as long as you trust the person with you, then you're always covered."

"Noted. I won't share your secret. I appreciate you trusting me with your back. Now, it's been a while since I've eaten here. What's his special now?"

"Today is meatloaf, mashed potatoes, gravy and rolls. Thank goodness we got here early because it sells out at lunch every week."

Instead of the waitress, the owner came over to take their order.

"War, welcome back. I wondered when you'd come in." Shaking War's hand, he turned to Remington. "I knew I'd see you. You only miss my meatloaf when you're out of town."

"Wouldn't miss it." She smiled. He had the best food, and the diner was a happy place.

"Remington said I can't miss the meatloaf, so you know I've got to try it."

"Good. We'll get that right out. Besides seeing you, War, I wanted to update you both. My niece's husband left her, and she's got those three little ones. Her parents are a waste of space so I'm going to go live with her and take care of her little ones. I've always wanted grandkids so I'm claiming them. I promised

Regina and Baron I'd give you guys first chance to buy the diner. You bring it to the table and let me know if you want to pursue it."

"Sure. I will. Thanks for letting us know."

War's voice was confident, but she'd seen the flash in his eyes. He'd been gone a long time and had no idea about the relationship between the MC and the diner. She couldn't decide if she wanted to be accommodating to this War who held the door open for her and had treated her as an equal or if she'd let him find out on his own. He had stated he hoped she'd teach him, so she really didn't have a choice.

As the owner walked away, War turned to her.

"Mom and Dad want the diner?"

The dismay in his voice had her taking pity on him.

"Regina loves to cook and most of his staff have been trained by her. He doesn't have the patience. She didn't want to compete with him, but she's dreamed of opening a place using the ingredients from the orchard and farm. I know she was a part owner before Ariel was born and he bought her share out. I believe there was some agreement that requires him to offer it to her first. I don't think she actively wants to be here every day but it's uncanny how she finds the right person for the job and in doing so, changes their lives."

Their food being dropped off put an end to their discussion as they both dug into the meatloaf. It was exactly how she loved it. A little crispy on the top crust with a moist, flavorful center. Once in a great while she'd put in an order and pick up a whole loaf to slice and have on sandwiches. There were a limited number for take-out, and she didn't want to do it too often. Everyone deserved to have this deliciousness.

"Forgive me if I moan but these mashed potatoes are almost as good as Mom's."

She tried not to giggle as he shoveled another huge spoonful in. He'd been away a long time. She couldn't imagine not having all her favorite things for that long plus, she'd never survive for long without her sisters.

"They're your mom's recipe. She improved on his because he came to Sunday lunch and basically promised her the world if she'd share how she made them."

He nodded but she didn't think he understood everything Regina had built. He'd left when he was eighteen and hadn't come back for any length of time. If she had to guess, he still viewed his mom as a homemaker, not realizing all Regina had done and built over the years. The orchard and vegetable gardens had continued to grow. If he didn't know about that, she wondered if she and Regina's secret project had come up. Not that it was secret from everyone. Her dad and sisters were in on it along with select ones in the MC. War and the guys would eventually know about it, but the project was only discussed in a secure location and only once a quarter. Their next get together was after she and Bear returned from their security detail.

"So, tell me, how is it being back?"

"Strange but good if that makes sense. The transition has gone well with Dad stepping down, but the MC has grown a lot over the years—like the security company. I had no idea about it."

"It's relatively recent so it might not have come up. I had the idea and went to Sarah since she's an accounting whiz. We put together a business plan and then approached Dad. Once we had his blessing, we talked with Baron and Regina. Then Baron took it before the brotherhood."

"Why Mom?"

His question threw her off a little but with him thinking it was only a security company, she could see how he'd be confused.

"We set up the business plan with forty percent of the profits to the brotherhood, forty percent to the bail bonds and twenty percent to some special projects we support or run. Regina is an amazing businesswoman and was interested in a couple of the special projects."

She didn't have a problem sharing the special projects with him but she, for sure, wasn't going to do it in a diner where anyone could overhear them. They were her babies, and she wasn't having them jeopardized because the wrong person heard something.

She answered his questions, wondering if he was turning over a new leaf in their relationship or if he'd flip the next time he saw her and she'd get the cantankerous ass who called her princess. She'd have to wait and see. She was a betting woman and right now, she'd bet on the ass coming back to visit.

Chapter Eleven

Remington was frustrated and the back of her neck was crawling. For the first time on a security detail, she was ready to leave a client high and dry. She'd never even considered it before, but this guy had all her senses screaming that nothing was as it seemed. Bear was currently walking the perimeter and checking exits for the second time tonight. They'd come to this location after the client had changed plans on them. They'd argued it would be harder to protect him at a location they hadn't previously vetted, but he'd insisted. Their contract didn't specifically prohibit the client requesting a change of venue, but he was the first. She'd vetoed his request to not have one of them within the penthouse. The little vein pulsing in his forehead let her know how displeased he was along with his screaming. Their contract did specify the client had to allow them within their personal space. Once she was done with this asshat, she'd be speaking to their attorney and having the language added for a change of venue only at the protection details' approval.

She wasn't sure what could have been missed. Each client went through a vetting process. He'd passed without any red flags. They had filled a couple positions in that department but with their screening process, they didn't usually miss things. She'd trained to notice the details and none of what she was seeing was adding up. She and Bear had traded glances multiple times. He was feeling it, too. Something was rotten, though they didn't have enough info to know what. The client had said he was getting threats. He was a political official at the state level with aspirations for a higher office supposedly home to campaign in his hometown but at this point, she was skeptical. They'd reviewed his threats and approved him for protection. She didn't get involved in politics besides voting but if this guy was ever on a higher office ballot, she might change her mind. The thought of him in charge of anything substantial for the country was frightening.

Due to his office, they were dressed in suits to blend in with his group. She texted Bear to grab their vests from the monitoring room when he came up. The longer she thought this through the more her skin crawled, screaming at her the danger was high. Their monitoring room was set up next door because although the asshat had given in on them having one of them within the room, he'd refused to allow their equipment in. Most clients jumped at the added protection. Just another tic for her what the fuck column.

She opened the door at Bear's radio announcement, he was outside the door. She yanked off her jacket, strapping the vest on, situating her holsters for easy access. Most protection details, she wore her single holster, but every minute was making her more anxious. She was always calm and collected whether it was security or skips. Sure, her adrenaline spiked during jobs, but she'd never felt this overwhelming dread.

"Thoughts?"

She and Bear weren't on their first detail. His demeanor when he walked in was telling her he was right there with her. Something was rotten in Dodge City tonight.

"He calls us because he's getting threats but then doesn't follow our requests. We move to a second venue, which has even less security, yet he seems happy to be here. Plus, he's stopped his conversation multiple times when I walk in the room like he's hiding something. The contract states everything we hear is confidential unless it's illegal so why be so scared to let us hear what he's saying?"

She agreed. Nothing made sense.

"Okay. I think we need to both be in here with him. I'm considering calling in extra manpower."

"I agree. I think if nothing else, you need to notify HQ something's off, so they'll be ready. He can kiss my ass if he thinks he's throwing me out."

She nodded and waited until Bear had walked in with the client. She texted into their detail text.

Code Phoebe – Client and detail at secondary location.

Confirmed. After previous change, backup was moved to your location. Holding on main floor of your location unless directed otherwise. ETA 4 minutes if you request help.

She'd notified them earlier when they changed the location but hadn't felt the need to state how off everything felt. Obviously, her sisters had heard something. She and Bear were the only detail who was supposed to be in Dodge City tonight. They must have moved backup closer in the last two hours. She clicked into her app which gave her camera views from their equipment. She had views off all entrances to this floor. One of the reasons she hadn't wanted to move to this hotel is their penthouse wasn't a secure floor with the elevator only going to that level with a key. The penthouse floor also allowed access to anyone because the stairs to an outdoor patio were on the same floor.

She clicked through the feeds again, pausing on the door to the outdoor patio.

"Bear, Code Ross. Three imminent."

Her security app picked up her voice with their distress call of Code Ross which notified her base everything's not fine, imminent danger, but she hit her distress button just in case. You couldn't have too much backup. Her distress button would notify local law enforcement in addition to her team.

Bear moved their client to the place they'd deemed the most secure, which was the bathroom. She moved back to a protected place where she had line of sight. She clicked to their balcony. At least they were only assaulting from one direction. Grabbing her bag, she pulled out her secondary guns. She hoped and prayed they wouldn't be needed but she'd be prepared for anything.

A loud bang heralded the lock being blown. These weren't your average guys if they had access to explosives to blow the door. She waited until the door opened then started firing from behind cover. She ducked, closed her eyes and covered her ears as a flash bang was thrown in. Then, she popped out from the side, firing toward the door.

Her detail text beeped, and *Code Chandler* appeared on her watch. Friendlies coming in and backup imminent. She caught a glimpse of one of the intruders in the mirror over the bar, coming toward her position. She paused, waiting for him to come a little closer, then slid around the end of the couch, popping up and shooting until he fell. She slid over to check he was down permanently, staying behind the couch, then checked the room. No one was in the room with her, so they'd already made it to the bedroom.

War sipped his iced tea while watching Winnie and Scoop watching a computer. Two hours ago, Sarah had notified War that she wanted him and at least three of the guys hanging out at a bar with Winnie and Beth in Dodge City. When he'd questioned her, she'd said she had a bad feeling and wanted backup close by. Winnie, along with a couple of security employees, would meet them there. If everything was fine, they could return to town or spend the night in the hotel. Protocols were no cuts, just blend in at the bar.

They'd been hanging out for about a half hour, and he had to admit, something felt off. He had the same feeling tonight that he'd had the night of the fire, which had spurred his decision to quit the department. He walked over to Scoop and Winnie. Flick was hanging near the door, leaning against the wall watching the parking lot. For once, he wasn't quoting any movies. He was feeling it, too. He was focused on what was next. Cannon had been cracking his knuckles and neck almost continuously. Everyone knew something was rotten.

"Anything?"

Winnie shook her head. "No, but everything inside me is screaming something's off. Let's move next door to the bar in the hotel. I want to be closer."

He paid their tab and before they walked in, he paused.

"Put on your vests. You can stage in the bar, but I want to be closer. I'm heading to the stairwell and staging on the floor below."

They split into two teams, going up both sets of stairs. His skin was crawling as if hundreds of spider legs were running everywhere. It was the same feeling that had saved his life in the military multiple times. He clocked the floor numbers as they ran up the stairs. Two levels to be there. As he passed the next level, his security text went off.

Code Ross, Three imminent.

He listened to everyone in his ear as they cleared their areas. He spotted the lone man left to guard the entry. Shooting, he clipped him as someone else on the team's bullet spun him when it hit his shoulder. In what seemed like minutes but was only seconds, they had him subdued and entered the apartment. The smell of gunfire hung in the air, but it was quiet. Too quiet. Winnie broke off to check the status of the downed man near the bar. She shook her head.

He motioned he was taking the lead into the bedroom. No one in the room—he moved toward the bathroom.

Bear Code Joey. 2 targets neutralized. Holding bathroom.

"War coming in!" he yelled. He didn't particularly want to be shot tonight.

Opening the door, Remington was holding a towel against Bear's side. The bullet must have hit at a perfect angle, completely missing his vest. The client was cowering in the tub. Remington's other hand had her gun leveled at one of the intruders. He'd taken a couple hits. His face was bloody, and Remington had cuffed his hands behind him.

"Flick, get in here."

Although they all had basic medical knowledge, as an EMT, Flick was best suited for the job. Remington moved once Flick had him and Winnie slid into Remington's place. Even though he was furious she'd been in danger, he was impressed with Remington. She'd obviously had an injured partner and still managed to keep the client safe and take him down.

She walked over to War. Glancing around, she nodded. "Thanks for the backup. Flick, you'll go with Bear. Cannon, would you and Scoop stay with our client in the bedroom? War will be with me. Winnie, you're on police detail."

She didn't wait for anyone to answer her. She reached down, grabbed the guy and hauled him to his feet. Pulling him out into the front room, she glanced around. Smirking, she walked over to the balcony. She glanced at the security person who'd come with them.

"You're on law enforcement detail. I don't want anyone bothering me."

"Got it, boss."

Following her out to the balcony, he was intrigued by her demeanor. What did she plan on doing?

She shoved the guy into one of the chairs and stood in front of him. Glaring at him, she let him fidget a little. After having her watch him for a couple minutes, he couldn't stand it.

"What?"

She walked closer.

"I'm going to ask you questions and I expect honest answers. I'm not in a happy mood after you shot one of my detail."

"I didn't shoot him," he protested.

"You might not have fired that shot but you fired tonight. Now, what was your objective?"

He was impressed with her technique. Most people asked who the person was and immediately put people on the defensive. She was asking about his actions.

"I can't say."

"I get that. You think you have some allegiance to whoever paid your bill. It's admirable but you seem like a smart guy so I'm going to give you your options. Option A—you tell me what I want to know, and you walk out of here. I won't even touch you. Option B—well, let me show you."

Remington grabbed his arm, pushing him toward the balcony railing.

"That's a long way down. I wonder how fast a body would be falling by the time it crashed into that cement. Do you think the person would live and if so, would they ever walk again?"

She shoved him back in the seat, his eyes skittering back and forth to Remington. Her little explanation had scared the little shit, but something seemed to be scaring him more.

"I'll ask again. What was your objective?"

"He'll kill me."

Remington looked at him and then peered over the balcony again, not saying a word. Her eyebrow quirked quizzically at him, waiting for his answer. In the light from the moon and the darkness, even he had to agree she looked capable of tossing the guy over the railing.

"How will he know?" she questioned.

The guy shrugged his shoulder toward the room where their client was waiting. Remington glanced at him, and he knew they had the same what the fuck look on their face.

"Change of plans. I'm going to send you out with War, and he'll take you downstairs. I'm going to go in and make a big deal about you refusing to talk. I'm going to let it slip we're taking you directly to the jail. War will take you somewhere safe and you'll be telling us everything. Deal?"

He nodded. "He won't just kill me if he thinks I talked. He'll go after my younger brother."

"Okay. Do what I say, and we'll protect your brother, too, if he's innocent. Now, play your part. When you go in, War's going to give you a shove. Make sure you call me a name or something that would be in your vocabulary."

War pulled him out of the chair while Remington was typing. His phone beeped.

Client compromised. War taking witness to secondary. Keep client unaware.

As he walked through the room, he did his part exactly as she'd directed.

When the client asked what she'd found out, she yelled nothing then asked him if they'd told him everything. Her acting skills impressed him because she had tears forming in her eyes about Bear while apologizing to the client about allowing this to happen. The guy was eating it up.

He'd imagined he'd be coming to her rescue when they breached the room, but Remington had surprised him with her abilities. The girl he knew had changed into a capable badass woman and if he was being truthful with himself, it was a fucking turn on.

Now, he had to follow the directions and get this guy taken somewhere so they could get some answers. He'd learned a lot about the security company in the last week. They had security protocols over security protocols to make sure they knew who they were protecting. What was this guy hiding and how did he get past them?

Chapter Twelve

Remington walked out of the hospital bathroom. She'd grabbed her extra clothes and a nice nurse had directed her to a place to clean up. Bear was in surgery. She'd moved the client to one of their safe houses along with one of the security details. She'd taken his phone on the ruse that it could be tracked. She was going to let Scoop and Sarah work their magic and find out what was going on.

Their shooter had been a fountain of information. They'd been hired to take her and Bear both out by the client who had engaged their services. She originally wasn't on the schedule for this client, but he'd demanded he wanted the head of the security company. The client would be kidnapped and then let go later after a supposed ransom payment. The shooter hadn't known the reasons why. He'd agreed because he'd been laid off and they'd threatened his younger brother.

She wasn't sure whether she was going to scream or cry. The relief she'd felt when War walked through the door had been immediate. She wasn't alone. Once things had calmed down, she imagined walking down the hall and having his arms wrap around her. She could be strong but sometimes, she wanted someone to share this life with. To have a shoulder to lean on. Not someone to stand in front of her but beside her. She turned the corner, and the object of her dream was leaning against the wall.

His eyes catalogued her for injuries. He saw whatever was in her eyes or on her face and he knew what she needed. He slowly opened his arms, tilting his head questioningly. She might regret this tomorrow but for a moment—this moment—she needed him. Walking closer, she could smell the musk of his exertions earlier and his unique smell. She wasn't even sure why it was a smell that comforted her, but it was. She wasn't questioning it tonight. Sliding her arms around his waist, she laid her head on his shoulder and relaxed against him. For now, she didn't need to think about what was next and how to fix this. She was a woman taking comfort from a man.

His arms slid around her, one pulling her flush against him while the other rubbed her back. His head tilted closer, his firm lips finding her forehead, pressing a kiss against her. She stood there with the hospital sounds all around them, finding comfort in his arms. In a second, she'd focus on what was next but right now, they weren't enemies. Co-workers, colleagues, whatever she wanted to call it. It was comfortable after a shared experience.

"It's been a long time since I've felt that fear but I'm going to admit something."

He paused and she waited for him to go on. When he didn't say anything, she tilted back to see his face. He smiled and his eyes were twinkling.

"Honey, you're nobody's friggin' princess."

She smiled at his tone. She leaned up, sliding her hand through his hair to tilt his face down. She slid her lips close to his ear. "And don't you forget it."

She bussed his cheek. "Thanks for being there. We need to check on Bear and then figure out how the hell this happened and why. We have so many protocols and we missed something.

Nothing makes sense. I have too many whys and not enough answers."

"I agree. Let's go." His arm slid off her waist and it surprised her how much she missed it. She wasn't ready to allow him a free pass for his behavior but in this moment, she'd let her guard down. Everyone deserved a second chance and maybe he'd changed his behavior. Maybe they could be co-workers without his animosity. His fingers entwined with hers as they walked down the hall. His approval felt right, and she wasn't sure why but for now, she wasn't going to question it.

She had too many other things to worry about, like how and why the client, who on the surface seemed like a political individual who wanted what was best for his country, would want her and Bear dead.

Tonight was one of those times it paid to work with your sisters who knew everything about you. Sarah had either heard something in her voice or had the same bad feeling. Things could have ended so differently if they hadn't had backup. If the guy at the door would have eventually come in, she would have had to defend them and it's possible even handcuffed, having to turn her attention toward the new shooter could have changed tonight's outcome.

Walking in the room, she spied Rascal, Regina and Baron already in the waiting room. She walked over and hugged Rascal.

"Sorry I didn't keep him safe."

Rascal shook his head. "Girlie, you and I both know you're the reason he made it to the hospital. You kept pressure on the wound and were ready to defend you both. Hell, for keeping my boy okay, your next tattoo is free."

She smiled at his teasing. She hadn't paid cash for a tattoo from him in years. She'd brought him pumpkin bread the first time she went in. After that, he'd only tattoo her if she brought him four loaves of it. She'd never actually paid for any of her tattoos in cash. When Roam had found out about the pumpkin bread, he'd asked for babysitting services in exchange.

"Do you know anything yet?"

"No. The nurse said they've taken him in to surgery and either she or the doctor would update us when they had more information."

The doors to the stairs banged open as Winnie rushed into the room. Winnie was always happy go lucky and could find the positive in any situation. Tonight, she looked scared and worried. She'd wondered if her sister was interested in Bear and her demeanor right now was a huge red flag waving, *I'm scared for my man.*

"How is he?" she barked.

"In surgery. Come here, darlin'," Rascal held an arm out and tugged her close as tears filled Winnie's eyes. His arms enveloped her and patted her back. "I'm sure he'll be his pessimistic, difficult self in no time at all."

Bear was pessimistic but his pessimism came out in the best ways on a security job. He thought through all the worst-case scenarios and then they planned for them. Unfortunately, they'd never had a client request a secondary location and it was the one scenario they hadn't considered.

"Family of Benton Carter?" a doctor questioned.

"I'm his dad," Rascal answered.

"He came through great. No vital organs were damaged, but he'll be kept overnight for sure. We'll be watching for infection, but I see no reason he shouldn't make a full recovery. He'll be in recovery then you'll be able to see him when he's in his room."

"Thank you, Doctor."

Now that she knew he was okay, she was heading to do a little more research into their client and ask some questions of the shooter. This wasn't happening again, and she was finding out why he'd ordered it.

Chapter Thirteen

Remington gathered her notes and walked into the darkened gym. Besides hunting down all the clues regarding their botched security detail and digging into the politician, she'd been busy getting their quarterly report ready.

They were meeting at the gym this time. The meeting place changed and to ensure they weren't all seen the same place each quarter, two people always attended virtually. Some people might think their plans were overreacting, but each choice was made to grow this project as safely as possible. Tonight, Winchester and Jesse were virtual. Winchester had volunteered, which was unusual. She always whined when it was her turn. She'd been running more than normal, which was usually her way of working through a problem. Winnie had the most positive personality of all of them, but she was also a little introverted, though when she was ready, she'd brief her sisters. Remi had considered every angle and knew tonight had the power to be explosive. War, Bear, Cannon, Flick and Scoop would be learning about their projects.

She'd had trouble focusing on her pet project because they still didn't know why they'd been targeted. Their client had gone back to Topeka, and she'd closed out the contract. As far as he was concerned, he'd gotten away with everything. The shooter and his brother had been helped and would be unavailable for retaliation.

She was nervous and it all came down to War. She hadn't been able to quit thinking about his arms around her and his lips against her forehead. He may have meant it as comfort, but it had stirred every daydream she'd ever had about him. Even when she was her angriest, she'd still been attracted to him. She'd dreamed of someone strong to stand beside her and he'd always been the ideal. Of course, in every dream, he'd either kept his mouth shut or he'd been appreciative of her.

She wasn't getting any younger, but she hadn't found anyone who made her want more than short term, except War. He made her consider the future, but she wasn't trusting her judgment. She'd been hyper aware, and the adrenaline had been leaving her system. She might have imagined their connection because of the emotions coursing through her.

She clicked the lights on and focused on her report. She'd see what everyone said. It was up to all of them how they perceived what they'd built. Whether he supported her or not, she was having her dreams.

She paused, waiting for the guys' reactions. She'd rushed through the report because of the nervousness of what the guys would say. Without knowing Cannon, Flick or Scoop very well, she was watching War and Bear. Bear started to speak a couple times then paused. His pessimistic nature was running multiple worst-case scenarios before he responded.

"I just want to make sure I have this correct. Kathryn's Wings is basically a clandestine part of the security company that's never advertised but you help victims of human trafficking, sexual abuse and domestic violence. Even going so far as to find jobs, housing, basically whatever the victim needs."

"Yes, but we call them survivors because they've survived and are taking the next steps to a better future."

She was proud of Kathryn's Wings. They'd started small but had helped over sixty individuals in the first eighteen months. They'd named it after her mom because they'd wanted to honor how she'd helped people when she was alive. She wasn't sure why War's opinion mattered so much to her, but it did. She'd view him differently if he couldn't see the possibilities of what they'd started and built. She wanted to share this dream of hers with him.

"It's amazing. You all saw a problem and worked to make a difference. This is why we left law enforcement and you found a way to help those who weren't getting what they needed. I'm fucking excited to be a part of this. I'm stunned at how much you all have accomplished in such a short amount of time."

His smile and nod at her had her swallowing back tears. She was strong and wasn't showing how much his approval meant to her but to know he supported her meant the world. She saw so much pain and suffering in her job. To know they were making a difference one person at a time and that he recognized it gave her an approval she hadn't realized she was seeking.

"I agree. Count me in." Bear's lips almost tilted up in a small semblance of a smile. She already had a flash drive so he could review their procedures. Mr. Worst-Case Scenario would be perfect to fine tune their security measures. There were never too many fail safes. He was moving a lot better in the last month since the shooting.

"I'm excited about the possibilities and I'm willing to help in any way I can," Scoop said.

"Me, too. It's like we're going to be living the movies *The Eraser, Rambo: Last Blood,* and all Liam Neeson's movies combined. Count me in." Flick's comments had everyone smiling.

"I'm in and just in case anyone needs reminding—I'm also proficient in explosives. You know, if it's ever needed for anything," Cannon offered while grinning at the group.

"Well, we haven't needed that skill yet, but I'm pleased you're all on board. Now, let's hear the updates on financials."

She'd already reviewed the financials but everyone else needed to know where they were at. Since they didn't have a facility, their costs were dramatically less plus she didn't need manpower to protect a building. Not that a building was bad but being in such a small town, they'd known any type of place would be under scrutiny. With their offices all over the state, they had connections and moved people so their abusers couldn't find them or if they'd been taken from families, they helped them get back to them. Besides their safe houses for the security business, they had a second set which was only used for survivors. A Kathryn's Wings staff member lived in the residence and was ready to receive anyone at any time. She was proud of what they'd built in such a short time.

She couldn't stop worrying about why the politician had targeted them. Not just the security company but the MC. What did he have to gain by it? Everyone had motives and his were still unclear. Once they got more information maybe something would come to light. Until then, she'd have to be satisfied they'd fulfilled the contract. He'd tried to renew for another two weeks but she cited lack of manpower to be able to adequately protect him. He raised his voice and wanted to speak with the owner. When she replied he was, he'd huffed and hung up on her.

Feeling eyes on her, she glanced around the room. War was smiling at her. Wow! She might need to go change her underwear because he was warming every part of her. Scowling he was sexy but that smile with his full lips had her wanting to drag him off somewhere alone, throwing caution to the wind.

War had come into the meeting wondering what the secret project was they were discussing. He had to admit to himself he'd been condescending in his thoughts even if he hadn't voiced them. He'd figured they had some small project. He was ecstatic he'd kept his mouth shut. Remington, her family and the MC had built an organization. Their network they'd built was huge and he was fucking impressed.

It was exactly what he'd been looking for when he left the police force. A place to make a difference without all the rules he had to follow. Remington was beautiful any day but when she spoke about her passion project—she was radiant. The spark in her eyes and hand gestures communicated how much it meant to her.

He was feeling a little guilty how he'd treated her when they'd first reconnected. He'd been an ass who was acting like he was still in high school.

Even though he'd never admit it to anyone else, he'd always had a thing for her but with her dad being in the MC, she'd been off limits. Looking back, he'd been embarrassed he'd ruined her day but hadn't been able to shut up.

You'd think once he got back and was an adult, he would recognize his behavior as asinine, but it had taken his twin sitting down and asking him why he was acting like an eighteen-year-old around her instead of a man. Self-examination had sucked. Roam's words had pounded in his head until he'd finally taken a ride to clear his head.

Whatever crazy dynamic they had going on when they were younger didn't have to continue on now. As he'd parked his bike outside, he'd concluded he needed to spend time getting to know the Remington she'd grown into, not the one he'd thought he'd known.

"Okay. If there aren't any questions, we're good."

He waited to see if Remington would acknowledge him, and they could talk. She covertly glanced at him while she was finishing picking up her stuff. He'd be patient and wait her out.

"I don't have any questions, but I want to reiterate how impressed I am with what you've built."

He watched her think through his words for any hidden meaning. He needed to work on building a good working relationship with Remington because everything he'd done so far hadn't helped.

"Thanks." Her husky voice had him thinking of things he'd love to do to her.

"So, fight night is coming up again," he questioned.

"Yes, are you wanting a rematch?"

"No, I was hoping to attend it unscathed this time. I figured I'd just watch. You busy then or maybe I could take you out to eat on Thursday?"

He wanted to make amends and spending time with her wouldn't be a hardship. Everything about her called to him, even her strength. The fact she'd starred in his dreams last night had him rethinking everything he believed about her. Despite her making him fume during most of their interactions, he also wanted to slide his hand into her ponytail, turn her face toward his and claim her full lush lips. He was half hard thinking about how she'd looked in his dream above him, riding him.

"Why?"

Not the answer he expected but he could understand her reticence.

"Man, you don't ask the easy questions. Easy answer is we need to work together, and I've done a fantastic job of fucking up our working relationship before it even started."

"What if I don't want the easy answer?"

Her biting her lip as she asked the question had him glancing around the room, verifying everyone had left. He stepped closer, seeing her eyes widen. Did Remington have the same thoughts about him? After holding her in his arms, he couldn't get her off his mind. He slowly reached toward her hair, sliding his hand into the ponytail, cataloguing each response she had.

"Then I'd tell you I can't get the feel of you in my arms off my mind. I wonder what you'd taste like."

A slight shiver told him Remington wasn't immune to him. Leaning closer, he gave her seconds to back away. When she didn't, he claimed her lips, realizing her tongue tangling with his and having her in his arms was exactly what had been missing.

Her arms wrapping around him had him tugging her flush with him. His cock nestled against her, proclaiming everything he wanted to do with her. Backing her up against the table, he grasped her ass, lifting her onto the table. Remington opened her legs, making a place for him. He nestled in, not caring who might walk back in.

She was better than he'd imagined. Her taste, her scent, the sweet sounds she was making as he caressed her breast through her clothes, tweaking her hard nipple.

"Remington, are you locking up?"

Winnie's voice had Remington rigid in his arms.

"Yes, I'll be right there."

She scooted back a little, pulling her arms from around him. He hoped, no, prayed she wasn't regretting their kiss. He'd never felt that response from a woman before.

"Dinner Thursday?"

He really hoped she said yes. If she didn't, he'd be doing some investigating and planning because what he'd found with Remington was something he'd never had before. The way she caught fire in his arms had him wanting to tear her clothes off and not leave their bed for a week. And there was going to be a *'their'* bed.

"Yes."

The word was short and quiet, but he'd fucking take it. He'd been worried she would back out after their kiss. Now, he'd have to figure out a spectacular first date because he wasn't that guy who planned perfect dates but for Remington, it had to be perfect. He didn't want to give her any ammunition to keep him away. He had some ideas, but he might need to do a little recon to find out her likes and dislikes.

It had only taken a couple of hours for Remington to start regretting saying yes to War. There was a thin line between love and hate—sometimes you couldn't help yourself. It's like ice cream—you hate what it does to your hips, but you can't resist it either. His taste and touch had overwhelmed her, and she hadn't been able to resist. She'd been lying in bed when she finally admitted to herself one kiss and touch from War had blown every sexual encounter away. If his kiss was that explosive, what would it be like when she had him? And she would have him. She wasn't denying herself the pleasure but there would be ground rules.

He could be in charge in the bedroom sometimes because she had no doubt, he could rock her world but in real life, she wanted a man to stand beside her. Whether this lasted a night or longer, he'd need to understand she wasn't changing for anyone. Sure, if they decided they wanted more then there was the little give and take in a relationship that she'd be up for, but giving up her job or her passion with Kathryn's Wings wouldn't happen.

If and when she decided to have children, she'd curtail some of her activities because she'd never endanger a baby, but she was just as much a protector as he was. The War she was familiar with didn't strike her as the type of man who would want someone as opinionated as she was.

She'd have to wait and see what he did. Maybe he had a little more depth than she thought. She might regret saying yes but if she didn't take the chance, she'd never know if what she imagined in her dreams was possible. Tomorrow, she needed to focus on helping Winnie with the matchups for fight night and see where they were at on the motivation for their client wanting them dead. Then, review the security schedule for the next week.

The date might be a good break. Her dad was constantly harping on her and her sisters, they needed to take time for themselves. He had dreams of them all finding men who would give them what he and her mom had. She wanted the love of a good man, but she'd also seen what losing her mom did to him. Sometimes she saw a wistful look in his eyes. She was positive he was imagining her mom with them. Remington still missed her, but her dad still had good years in his life, and she didn't want him alone. She wasn't sure she'd ever vocalized that to him, though. She and her sisters should but she might wait awhile. Bringing up relationships would invite him to give his opinion on the state of her life and she wasn't sure she wanted that.

Chapter Fourteen

War paused in the doorway, relishing the yeasty smell of dough. It brought back so many memories from growing up. His mom had the kitchen island prepped for her next project. Her smile when she saw him walking in had him hurrying to grab her up and spin her around. He bussed a big smooching kiss on her cheek.

"Love you, Mama."

He loved the smile his words put on her face. When she smiled, he'd always thought she was like this ray of sunshine, beaming across them, lighting their way.

"Love you, too. You're just in time to help me. Wash your hands."

When his Mama directed, he listened. He washed his hands then waited for instructions.

"We're making apple tea rings and cinnamon tea rings this morning."

It had been forever since he'd had his mom's tea rings. She alternated the fillings depending on what she had on hand and who she was making it for. They all had their favorites. His was cinnamon with pecans. He got to work rolling out the dough, and then placing the filling exactly where his mama had taught, then rolling and pinching it to form the ring. He finished a little after his mom and covered his to rise for forty minutes.

She handed him a cup of coffee and pulled a warmed cinnamon roll from the microwave, leading him to the table.

"Not that I don't love having you help me in the kitchen, but you seem a little preoccupied. Normally, you'd be chatting the whole time and you haven't said a word. What's going on?"

What did he tell her and how much? She'd like nothing more than for him and Remington to fall in love and live happily ever after but he also didn't want to get her hopes up.

"I have a date set for tomorrow and I'm trying to figure out what to do."

"Hmmm."

Regina took a sip of her coffee while he felt like she was scrutinizing him under a microscope.

"I want to make it special but not sure which way to go."

She nodded and nudged his cinnamon roll closer. He never let his mama's cinnamon rolls just sit there. They were usually scarfed down in three to four bites. He cut off a piece and dug in. The sweet taste of the cinnamon, brown sugar and vanilla brought back the times they'd sat at this very table hashing out any problem he had going on. When he was younger, he'd never doubted that his mama or dad would be able to help him sort through any issue. If Baron wasn't over at the gun range, he'd be right there beside his mom.

"Tell me about her. What do you like about her?"

"She's strong, capable and isn't a pushover. She's gorgeous, of course, and I can't get her out of my mind. Loyal. She'd do anything for her family and those she considers family."

Regina nodded with a little grin on her face. Until he spouted the words, he hadn't realized he was going to share so much. His mama had always been an excellent interrogator. So many times, he, Matt, and Bear had thought they were getting away with something and boom—one of them would spill because they couldn't withstand her interrogation. It was done in a sweet, unassuming way until she pulled the words from you.

"She sounds special, so you don't want any run of the mill date."

He nodded and shoved another bite of cinnamon roll in. He'd had to up his workout routine for the number of sweets he'd added to his diet. He wasn't complaining because he'd missed his mama's food and her calm demeanor when he wasn't sure what to do.

He swallowed, sipped his coffee, and thought through what he wanted for her.

"She is and unfortunately, I was an ass when I came back so I also might have some apologizing to do."

"It sounds like you have a start. You want something unusual, something she likes to do. Maybe you need to think of something fun she'd like to do and couple it with something you think she wouldn't do for herself but might secretly want."

He knew by the smirk on her face she'd cottoned on to who he was talking about. What he never wanted to do was hurt his mama, but their date was about them. To see if what he wanted could be, but he didn't want his mama hurt if it didn't. He could be making the best decision of his life or the worst. He'd tried to think through all the scenarios but despite all the ways it could go wrong, he was compelled to try with Remington. The risk was worth the reward. He couldn't stand the thought of being twenty years down the road and by himself at the club and wonder what if.

Baron walked in, poured a cup of coffee, and nodded back toward the door. "Let's take a walk, son."

His mama patted his hand, leaning over to kiss his cheek. "Everything will be all right, War. The road to true love isn't a smooth path but if it was easy, we wouldn't cherish it as much."

Being away from home and especially once he'd started investigating his chief, he'd had to keep his guard up. With his family, he could relax and know they only wanted whatever was best for him. Baron had shown him over the years that being the MC president didn't mean you had to be unfeeling. If anything, it meant you were looking out for all your brothers and family.

Baron wouldn't think he was less than because his mama's words brought tears to his eyes. He stood up, wrapped his arms around her and picked her up. He kissed her forehead and let her down. "If I haven't told you lately, you are the best mother I ever could have asked for. Your strength taking a job at an MC clubhouse when we were little gave us the best family I could have dreamed of. Because of you, we got Baron for a dad and uncles who taught us how to be men. I love you, Mama."

Regina pushed him toward Baron. "Love you, too, son. Now go listen to Baron's advice."

Baron pulled Regina close, nuzzling her neck and then kissing her goodbye. He'd gotten used to knowing his parents had a very active sex life. Baron and Regina had no problem going off by themselves when they needed. He craved that connection with a woman—knowing what she wanted and providing it for her. Maybe Baron could give him some insight into a good relationship, though his mama was different from Remington. Baron protected his mama from everything. Remington wouldn't want to be protected. She'd be strong in her own right. He'd been judging Remington through the lens of the rookie he'd lost. His guilt over her death had skewed how he'd viewed Remington in her job. He wanted a clean slate with Remington and he hoped this date could be it.

Baron let him be quiet with his thoughts as they walked past a couple of new buildings toward the orchard and garden. He'd been home for a while and was a little ashamed he hadn't checked it out. When he left, his mom had a garden which helped the MC with fresh food. It had been small enough she could tend it by herself with one of the prospect's help.

They passed the last two buildings blocking the area. He paused and then looked over at what he had thought was a small garden. He wasn't sure it could still be classified as that. The orchard, which he last remembered as five trees, stretched in rows to the crest of the hill. He couldn't tell if it went farther. Rows of vegetables and fruits were laid out with enough room for pickers to take care of the plants. He followed Baron as he walked toward another area. Workers were already out tending areas. An irrigation system had been installed, which he considered a blessing. He remembered helping his mom drag hoses when they were still in high school, and that plot had been big by his standards. This area was big enough he'd call it a farm. How had Baron and the guys done all this?

"How?"

"Over the years with your mom's head for business, we've expanded. Not only does this provide all our produce, but she has also set us up as an organic farm and distributes to specialty stores within the state. Over the hill is where we raise our own beef. Currently, we don't have plans to expand because the area we have suits the needs of our family. It supplies the clubhouse, members who have houses, the diner in town and all the Franks family and employees. Everyone pays a fee and depending on what they've selected, they can either have it at their house or can pay to store it at our locker and processing plant. All of this is because of your mother."

He almost couldn't comprehend what she'd helped the MC build. He'd been seeing her through the eyes of a child. Maybe it was time he saw her for the amazing, strong woman she was.

"I have no words. It's astonishing."

Baron's arm pulled him close. "Son, it takes a strong man to recognize the strength in his woman. The hardest thing I've ever done is stand by and not solve things I perceive as issues for your mom. She is fully capable of handling just about anything she needs to. I think the woman you're interested in is a lot like your mom."

"I wouldn't have thought that before, but I do now." He shook his head at all he'd misunderstood over the years.

"The only time I stand in your mother's way is when the bullets are flying. Otherwise, I support her in whatever way she needs and watch her triumph."

Baron's arm and words reminded him of all he'd gained when Baron had adopted them and become his dad. "I hope I can be half the man for her that you are for Mom."

Baron's arm tightened. "I know you can, but strong women need a man who lets them know how special they are. Let's go figure out what you need to do. We're meeting Locks at the diner. If you're taking out a daughter of an MC member, you better get his blessing."

He grinned and followed his dad. Hopefully Locks would have some insight into how he could make tomorrow night special for Remington.

War looked back in at the diner at his dad and Locks enjoying the last of their coffee. He was glad they'd met, though Locks grilling him on his intentions when he really hadn't identified them himself had been hard. His questions had forced War to examine what he wanted out of the date. He wanted more—more information on if he'd imagined their connection and more time getting to know the woman Remington had become.

He created a group text with the numbers Locks had given him. He took a deep breath, wondering if he was really ready for their opinions.

War: Hey, I'd love your opinion on my date with Remington. I want to make it special. Do you all have any suggestions?

Sarah: Don't hurt her or I'll bury you on our land where no one will find your bones.

Winnie: I think she'd love if you kicked your own ass.

Jesse: She loves preppy guys. No beards at all. Think button ups with sweaters over their shoulders.

War: I'm not shaving my beard.

Jesse: I don't think you're trying that hard to get in our good graces.

Beth: No sex until at least the third date. It's Remi's rule to see if guys are worth the time. Show her how special she is and that she's worth the wait.

War: No sex on the first date seems a little strict when we've known each other for years.

Sarah: We could have suggested castration. No sex for three dates seems like a small price to pay to show her you're serious.

War: When and if we get married, are you guys going to feel bad about how you're treating me right now?

Beth: You seem pretty sure of yourself when you can't even figure out a first date for yourself. Does a dog know how to drive a car?

Why the hell was Beth asking about a dog driving a car? Her sisters were seriously in need of help. He was regretting trying to get their opinions, but Remi loved her sisters and he needed to figure out how to get along with them.

War: No, a dog can't drive a car.

Beth: There's your answer. No, we won't regret treating you this way. If you can't take it, you don't deserve her. Now remember, 3 dates until sex.

Her sisters were very opinionated but so far, they hadn't given him much help. He'd hoped they'd tell him the perfect date. Maybe they didn't want him to succeed. He needed them to realize he was serious, and this wasn't a joke. He fucking hated sharing feelings but if it helped her sisters open up to him, he'd do it.

War: Remington is special. I've never felt about anyone the way I feel about her. If this becomes her last first date, which I'm hoping it will, I want it to be memorable.

Jesse: Hey, give him a chance. Maybe he's not as stupid as we thought. He's asking our opinion and sharing feelings.

Winnie: She loves motorcycles, guns and being appreciated for who she is. If you can't see her for the awesome kickass woman she is, then cancel the date before tomorrow.

War: I'm not canceling.

Winnie: It sounds like you're serious. If you want it to be memorable, then take something negative and change the memories.

Sarah: Winnie, he needs to fucking figure this out by himself. Mr. MC President can surely figure out what would make her happy. It's not like he's still in high school.

Jesse: Follow your heart. If she is truly who you want, then do things that will make her happy, but I agree, follow the no sex before the third date. If you try before that, Remington will be upset.

Winnie: Yep, trying for earlier could completely ruin everything before that.

Sarah: On that point, we all agree.

Take something negative and make it positive. He could work with that, and he owned a gun range and shop. He had access to whatever he needed. The no sex until the third date with how explosive their kiss had been would suck but if that's what Remi needed to know he was serious, so be it.

War: You've given me some great ideas. I really appreciate your help.

Their replies ranged from thumbs up to don't fuck this up. He'd taken the first step toward his new normal with Remington and he had her sisters to thank for it. He needed to get planning. He wasn't screwing this up.

Chapter Fifteen

"I've got it!" Sarah screamed as she ran in with her computer. Her dad was missing their meeting but she and everyone else had too much going on to reschedule. Beth and she were discussing what she should wear on her date with War without knowing where they were going or what they were doing. She wanted to look nice but also didn't want to give him the wrong impression. She lived ninety percent of her time in motorcycle boots, jeans, shirt and jacket. She wasn't changing for him or any man. She wasn't the girly girl. Beth loved shopping for clothes, getting her nails done and being pampered sometimes. With her job as surveillance Beth had the perfect excuse for having a huge wardrobe. Remi wasn't like that. She enjoyed going to the gun range and checking out the latest guns, window shopping at the motorcycle store or stopping at the small bookstore that had recently opened in town.

"You've got what?"

Sarah sat down and slid the computer where she and Beth could see. "Vanilla Swirl and I have been working on connections between the client and either the MC, bail bonds, the security company or Kathryn's Wings. We went back over all our survivors and even checked where they are now. We found a small thread."

She waited for Sarah to continue. "Are you waiting for a pat on the back? Good job. Now tell me."

Sarah turned to Beth, giving her a look of what the fuck.

"Remi's nervous about her date. Cut her some slack. She's being a little short with everything."

"Got it. Do you remember survivor number five? We almost didn't help her."

Remi glossed over Sarah's ever-changing nicknames for Scoop and thought about number five. She remembered her all too well. Her story checked out, but something had seemed off the whole time. In fact, they'd been so concerned they hadn't used any of their safe houses. Sarah had found an Airbnb at Remington's request and used it until she moved on. She hadn't wanted to deny anyone, but something had set every sense tingling when she was around her.

"Yes, why?" Beth asked.

"When we checked on her, she seemed off. She wasn't even remotely close to where we had placed her. Our policies dictate that any movement on their part within the first year needs to be sent to the message board. It's a safeguard to make sure something hasn't made them run. Any guesses where she was?"

Remington's stomach swirled. Why did this feel like she didn't want to know the answer?

"Where?"

Sarah pointed to the computer. "In Topeka, working at our client's office. When Butter Pecan checked a couple things, he found paystubs showing she'd worked for his company prior to us relocating her."

Remington couldn't figure out what would have had her coming through as a survivor. She'd been through month three because they'd started slow.

"Keep digging. Double check everything we believed about her. I want to know everything about her and why we didn't catch this when she came to us. That's a huge hole in our process. Sarah, good catch."

"You can thank Mint Chocolate Chip. We were both working it, but he was the one that did some fancy maneuvering to get the pay stubs."

For a little bit, she quit worrying about her date and concentrated on their security issues. She hated puzzles she couldn't figure out and there were too many open threads. The biggest issue she had was if he wanted them dead before, was he going to try again? They didn't have enough to have the MC go on lockdown or institute their next security protocol, but she had that itch on the back of her neck telling her to buckle up, something was coming for them. Her phone buzzed with a text. She'd assigned a motorcycle revving to War's text messages which was an improvement over her previous "I'm a loser" ringtone.

War: Looking forward to tomorrow night. Wear your favorite boots, jeans, and jacket. I'll be picking you up on my motorcycle if you're good with that.

Wow! If she didn't know this was War's number, she'd assume someone else had taken over his body. Asking if she was good riding on his motorcycle was nice. Getting to wear her favorite clothes helped relax her a little.

Remi: Perfect. What time?

War: 5. I'll see you then.

Maybe tomorrow would be the start of something different for them and she wouldn't regret saying yes. It had been forever since she'd anticipated going out on a date. She did want to look her best and hated trying to figure out what to wear. Heck, she had the same suit in three different shades of grey to make dressing for the security company easier.

"Okay, Beth, you win. You can do my nails as long as it's clear polish or a light color. You can also pick out the jeans and my top. I want to look nice but still want to look like me."

"Woohoo!" Beth yelled and jumped up, dancing around the room.

Jesse and Winnie walked in. "What is going on?"

"Remi's letting me do her nails and pick her top for her date. War won't know what hit him."

Jesse and Winnie just smiled at Beth's antics. She loved all her sisters with their quirks and all. She needed to get some work done if she was taking off tomorrow night. Her dad would scold her if he knew how many evenings she did work at home in front of her TV. She hoped War wasn't disappointed because she wasn't one to need to be out every night. She loved being home in the evening and relaxing. She wasn't a party all the time girl even when she was younger. She'd see. He might pick her up and turn into the asshole who called her princess and treated her as if she didn't matter. If that happened, she'd deal, but she was hoping tomorrow night was the start of something new for them.

Could he be someone who would see her for who she was? Would he expect her to change, or would he help her achieve her dreams? She'd never know unless she opened herself up a little to see. For the time being, she was going to give him the benefit of the doubt. Despite how much of an ass he'd been, whenever she pictured her ideal life, it was with him.

She hated being vulnerable, but War had the ability to destroy her if she opened herself up and he rejected her but that little part of her that still believed in fairy tales wanted him to see her for who she was and know she was exactly what he needed.

Chapter Sixteen

War checked over his bike. He'd had one of the prospects detail it today. He wanted everything perfect for their date. He'd learned a lot in all the conversations he'd had. He'd even spent time chatting with his twin. Of all the guys, he was the one that told him brother or no, if he hurt Remington, he'd be kicking his ass.

Bear walked in and sat down. He waited. Bear may be his best friend, but he also wasn't above telling him he was being an idiot. He hoped he wasn't here to discourage him from going out with Remington.

"Bike looks good. You've planned a good evening. You have one more thing before you go, though."

He glanced at his friend. The man who had dragged him through some of the worst times of his life and helped him survive. Arching his brow, he waited. He wasn't leaving until Bear said his peace and he had thirty minutes before he needed to leave to pick up Remington.

"You have to let the guilt go."

Let the guilt go. How did you let twenty years of regret and guilt go just because someone said so? Bear knew what had happened. He'd been there. War had failed and no one else was to blame. Guilt and regret had been his constant companions.

"Guilt keeps us from making the same mistake again," he replied. Bear's shake of his head irritated him. Why did he have to bring it up before his date? Like he didn't have enough on his mind tonight already.

"It wasn't your mistake. It was hers. I'd give anything to go back and not have you carry this burden."

He'd wondered over the years if Bear had felt as bad as he did. She'd only been his trainee because Bear had been injured and he'd been picked to complete her training. He remembered being so worried for his friend and furious that the captain had chosen him to take over her training. He'd read all Bear's notes. He'd been ready to request she be placed on disciplinary action for not following orders. Bear hadn't yet because she was the daughter of one of the captain's friends. He'd decided to give her the benefit of the doubt, which had been a mistake. The biggest mistake during his career in law enforcement. Her death was on him.

"It was mine."

"No, dumbass, it was hers. Despite all the training she was afforded, she always knew better. If she had been anyone else, she would have been gone before I got hurt. I listened to the captain and didn't boot her when I should have. It is my deepest regret because of what it caused for you, but you have to let it go. It has colored every decision you've made. You've judged every woman by the way she screwed you up. Remington deserves the man I know you are—not the one you judge yourself to be."

Bear made it sound so easy, but he'd carried the load a long time. He honestly couldn't remember a time when he didn't have the weight on his shoulders. He hadn't heard his friend string so many words together in forever.

"How?" he croaked.

Bear stood and walked over, pulling him into a hug. "You share it with her. I'm sure she'll help you shoulder the load.

Plus, I'm sure she's got stuff, too. You can't do the type of stuff we do without it leaving its mark. You deserve happiness."

He'd think about it. He wasn't sure he was ready to share the part of his life he was ashamed of. It was a freaking first date. He could just see spilling his guts over their dinner. What if she blamed him? Despite Bear's assurances, the guilt was still there.

"Thanks. I'll think about it."

Bear nodded and walked out as silent as he came in. Since Bear had been shot, he'd seemed different. His countenance hadn't changed but he almost seemed a little lighter sometimes. He grabbed the items he was taking, checking they were still wrapped as he slid them in his saddle bag.

He had a lot to think about and consider. Could he let go of the sins of the past? Remington did deserve the best of him. Maybe it was time.

He hadn't made any progress on letting go of the guilt on the drive. He hadn't considered how nervous he might be. The closer he got to their compound, the sweatier his hands were. He turned onto their drive, following Remington's directions leading him by the main house then around a curve. Five houses with huge differences in architectural style were linked by different paths and roads. She'd said hers was the smallest with the biggest porch. She hadn't exaggerated. Hers looked like a log cabin built on the prairie except she had a huge wraparound porch with comfortable furniture inviting someone to sit and stay awhile. He backed his motorcycle in and parked where the sign indicated. *Bikers parking. Cages in the back. Violators will meet an appropriate end.*

He was curious exactly what Remington considered an appropriate end. She didn't suffer fools lightly and anyone who could read should be able to follow the directions. He lifted the flowers out of his side bags, gently unwrapping them. He grabbed the bag with her other present. He hoped he'd chosen correctly.

He knocked on the door, glancing around. One of the houses was close enough he could see the curtains moving in the window. Someone pulled back the curtains and four hands waved at him. He smiled at her sisters keeping an eye out. Were they snooping or were they there to help Remington get rid of him if he was an ass to her?

Remington opened the door. She took his breath away. She'd always been beautiful, but he hadn't taken the time to look at her face. It was a little fuller than high school, but it made her face more interesting. Her eyes scrutinized him and widened when she saw the flowers and package. Her hair was down tonight and had him imagining grasping it, directing her mouth close to him. He handed her the flowers.

"You look beautiful tonight."

"Thank you. The flowers are gorgeous. Let me grab a vase then I'm diving into that bag because I love presents."

A leather sofa, loveseat and chair with colorful blankets were in the front room. She'd divided the space with the furniture, but it was open concept through to the kitchen. She brought the flowers and set them on the table by a chair, motioning with her hands to give her the bag.

"If it's not what you were wanting, you can exchange or return it."

Her hands untied the bow and had tugged the tissue paper out in seconds. Unwrapping her present, her smile widened. She jumped up, pulled him close and smacked her lips against his.

"I love it. I've had this on my list, but I didn't know it could be personalized."

He was glad she loved her bullet loader but the quick kiss she'd laid on his lips wasn't enough. He slid his hand into her hair, tugging her flush against him. Her curves against him had him wishing his jeans were a little bigger. He was surprised he had any blood left in his brain as he hardened.

"Your kiss was perfect but not nearly long enough," he whispered as he captured her mouth. Their first kiss had been good but he'd remember this one on their first date forever. The taste of her mint toothpaste, the feel of her mouth letting him in and contentment in his chest revealing she was his.

Remington didn't just let him take control, she had him wondering if they'd make it to dinner as they devoured each other. His breathing was heavy as he reluctantly pulled away.

"I'd like nothing more than to explore this more, but we have plans. I don't want us to miss them."

Remington nodded, grabbed her jacket, helmet and a small purse. Following behind him, she locked the door and slid her hair into a sheath.

"Seriously?" Remington huffed.

He glanced to see what had her irritated then laughed. In the time he'd been in the house, her sisters had been busy. They were on the front porch, a couple sitting in rocking chairs and a couple standing, leaning against the porch posts reminiscent of every western he'd watched. They were each holding a gun—not just any guns either. He saw a shotgun, an AR-15, a sniper rifle, and Beth had a hand crank 9mm gatling gun in front of her on a small table. One of them had taken a piece of plywood and spray painted *You hurt her, and no one will find the body.*

"I think it's sweet they're making sure I know there are consequences."

He waited for Remington to get on and slide close. He was curious if she'd wrap herself around him or if he'd need to tug her closer. He hadn't decided if having her on the bike would be a dream come true with her wrapped around him or if he'd be the hardest he'd ever been.

For the first time since he was back, he was ready for what was ahead. The kiss had cemented in his mind that Remington would be his.

Remington glanced around the room. He'd brought her to the clubhouse. Were they hanging with his brothers? She'd told him she didn't care what they did. She'd been dying to know what he had planned. Walking into the clubhouse, she noticed the lack of sound. She'd rarely been here when multiple sounds of pool balls, TV and brothers talking weren't competing for supremacy.

A table was to the side and set for an intimate dinner. War texted as he led her to her seat, waiting until she was situated before he took his.

"I picked here because this is the spot where I hurt you. I was a young guy who was too full of himself. I thought we'd make new memories here to replace the bad ones. I know we both loved the food and I wanted this to be a new start for us. We can't change the past, but we can step forward into the future, which is what I want with you."

One of the prospects visiting from their Texas chapter walked out with his cut on over a starched white shirt and pressed jeans.

"What can I get you to drink?"

She bit back a smile at his pad of paper and pen waiting for her choice.

"Whatever War is having."

He'd planned the date and with the care taken so far, she was sure he had figured out her favorite drinks.

"We'll take the drinks chilling in the fridge, and you can bring out the appetizers."

He almost looked like he was shaking as he scurried back to the kitchen. She arched her brow and War chuckled.

"I might have threatened him with a couple of things if he screwed this up."

"You don't want members that don't love the brotherhood and wouldn't do anything for each other."

War waited while their drinks and appetizers were placed by them. He immediately cut a piece of bread, buttered it, and placed it on her plate along with a couple of the appetizers before taking care of himself.

"I agree. Until the issues on the security gig with that jackass client you had, it's been relatively quiet for a while, but it never lasts. I need to know anyone who becomes a member will do whatever it takes to protect the family. A couple weeks after I was home, a prospect came up for voting to patch in. The day before Mom had told me he'd gone with her to pick up some supplies. He played on his phone, and she waited five minutes before he glanced up and saw her. Anything could have happened. We kicked him to the curb, but I'd been angry someone hadn't noticed it before, but I guess he hid it well."

She finished her potato skin and wiped her mouth. "We have a longer orientation process now because someone made it through a couple years ago and ran at the first sound of gunfire."

He chuckled. "I heard about your most recent orientation from Cannon. He said he laughed until tears ran down his face. He said he was surprised the guy didn't wet his pants. He was also irritated he didn't have the cameras running."

She laughed, remembering his terror as he ran through the course and she fired. He didn't know they were blanks but it gave her a good idea what he'd do during a confrontation. The prospect returned, clearing their dishes away and placing new ones. She looked at the food and then at War waiting for her response. Her favorite main dishes Regina made were in little containers so they could have a sampling of all.

"This was a lot of work for Regina."

War nodded. "I helped and had two prospects helping her. She pretty much sat and enjoyed her iced tea and directed. She only got up a few times when she thought one of us wasn't doing something correctly."

For him to take the time to cook her meal with all her favorites told her more than words War wanted this to be the start of something for them. He, once again, had servings of everything on her plate before he selected anything for himself.

"I've been gone a long time. Would you be up for twenty questions?" he asked, his voice hopeful.

War had done his research on her. That was the only way he knew she loved to ask questions to get to know people better on assignments.

"Sure." She savored the bite of mashed potatoes with gravy.

"Favorite activity in your free time."

"Riding my bike or binge reading. I'm gone so much I love to stay home when I can."

"Best thing that's happened since you've come back."

"Well, it's tied. Getting to know my niece and nephews and going out with you."

She was almost worried because they were getting along so well. Was this the new normal or would things change? His lips claiming her before they left had surprised her at how she'd felt. She'd always wondered if she'd like kissing a man with a beard. The feel of it against her lips had her imagining everywhere else she could feel it. Everyone before had just been a placeholder but when War had touched her, she'd known he was the one.

"What's your dream vacation?"

She didn't need to think about this at all. She had a vision board hidden in a closet so her sisters couldn't see it because it was too personal. She loved them but sometimes she didn't need them to know everything.

"Renting an RV and spending a couple weeks traveling to different places, enjoying the sights with no schedule."

They'd finished their meal and the prospect had cleared the dishes. War stood, holding his hand out.

"Dessert is waiting for us, and we each have time for one more question—so make it a good one."

He held her hand and he led her down the hall. She'd loved kissing him but if he thought she was jumping in bed in his room with Regina a couple of feet away in the kitchen, he was dead wrong.

He led her into a storage room with a ladder at the end. He crawled up, opened a hatch and then looked at her. "Dessert is up here."

He stepped up through and put his hand down to her. She stepped up the ladder, grasping his hand and letting him help her up. The sun was close to the horizon at dusk. They didn't need the twinkling lights that were on the roof to see but she loved them. She'd never realized the clubhouse had a roof you could get on. A fire pit was lit with a couple chairs around it. He waited until she sat down then handed her marshmallows on sticks. S'mores were her favorite. She wanted the marshmallow completely blackened where the inside was so gooey it stuck to your teeth.

"This is perfect."

His bright smile gleamed at her words.

"Last question for me. If you could have anything, where do you see yourself in three years?"

He'd hit on her dreams. He wasn't pulling any punches with his questions, but they had a lot of time to make up for.

"Dream me wants kids before I'm too old, a husband, a couple pets and my kids growing up with their cousins."

He nodded, taking his completely burnt marshmallow, placing it on the chocolate bar and squishing it between the graham crackers. He handed it to her. She took a bite thinking about what to ask him, settling on one that would tell her more about his character.

"What's your biggest regret?"

His eyes stared into hers, his forehead pursed in thought.

"One of mine is saying yes to Roam when he bet Bear and me that he could win at poker. We took that bet because Roam always sucked at poker. I still don't know how he won but he did."

"What happened?"

"He had bet us that he got to practice piercing on us if we lost."

She looked at his shirt to see if she'd maybe missed a nipple piercing. War was shaking his head.

"I wish it was a nipple piercing."

Now, she really wanted to see what Roam had done. She had her own Roam stories with piercings.

"It was one of the most uncomfortable experiences of my life having my brother holding my dick while he pierced it."

She snorted, then couldn't hold it in. Imagining her big, badass biker having to let his brother pierce his dick was too funny. Freaking hot but extremely funny. Since she had a piercing from Roam which he'd won the opportunity to do, she had a suspicion they'd both been had. He'd suckered all of her sisters with that bet. She could see him having a good night, but Beth was phenomenal at poker because she had an eidetic memory. She knew every card that was played and could figure the odds.

"Not even close to anything I had ever imagined except I have to ask—did he wear sunglasses while you played?"

War glanced at her, surprised. "Yeah, how'd you know?"

"He made a similar bet with my sisters and me. We have a monthly poker game as a staff get together. He's joined us a couple times and lost. When he bet us, he invited us to the clubhouse then claimed he had a migraine, and the lights were bothering him. Beth is super observant and noticed he only won when he wore the blue glasses."

"That lying card shark. I'm guessing since you were playing at the clubhouse, he supplied the cards."

At her nod, he grinned.

"Two things—I'm dying to know where he pierced you and how'd you like to get him back?"

She liked how he thought, and she hadn't been mad at Roam because she'd already been planning on getting a belly button piercing. Whether it was Roam or Rascal piercing her hadn't mattered to her.

War's eyes heated as she unbuckled her belt and unzipped her jeans. Pulling her shirt up, her breath sped up as he leaned forward. His hand reached toward the piercing then paused, his brow quirked. She nodded though she wasn't sure having War's hands on her up here where they were all alone was her smartest decision.

His finger moved the piercing to view it better. His warm breath heated her skin.

"A pistol? Very fitting with your job."

His finger slid up, caressing her waist as his hand pulled her closer. She swallowed as War's mouth came closer, his intent clear. She was crazy for considering something with him considering their history, but sometimes, she didn't want to be the oldest one, always following the rules. His lips claimed hers. Who cared about obligations when he was pulling her close?

With War, she didn't need to think, just feel. His breathing sped up as he nibbled her ear, trailing kisses down her neck.

"I owe my brother a thank you. Your piercing is fucking hot. I can't wait to lick it and you when I finally have you alone."

War had them moving at lightning speed and honestly, she wasn't complaining. She'd fantasized about him forever. She reveled in his touch and the heat he generated in her. When he pulled away, she was disappointed. She craved more of him, but the roof wasn't where she wanted him.

"I'd like nothing more than to continue but we have a couple more places." He stood up, holding his hand out to her. She started to pick up their mess. "Leave it. The prospects will take care of it."

She took his hand and let him lead her. He'd thought out and planned an evening she hadn't expected. Although she would have loved to see where his kisses led, she was a little excited about what else he'd planned.

Chapter Seventeen

War unlocked the door of the gun range. He'd been floored when Remington had asked about his greatest regret. He'd taken the easy way out, sharing about his piercing. Bear's words had rung in his ears, but he hadn't been ready to open up yet.

"Unusual first date but I have to admit, I'm intrigued," Remington commented as they made their way through the store. He picked up the bag Cannon had left for him and flicked on the lights as he walked into the range. He hoped he hadn't made a mistake. Even after all the intel he'd garnered on Remington, he was still a little unsure she'd appreciate what he'd done.

He handed her the bag, motioning for her to open it. Her lips widened in a grin, and she bounced on her toes a little when her hand wrapped around what was in the bag.

"You got me a gun?"

"Cannon said you were drooling over his and I wanted something for you to remember our first date by."

"You've already done too much. I should say I can't take it, but I can't. Can we try it out?"

He led her to lane one where Cannon had set up his requests. A stack of range bullets fitting her new pistol waited along with eye and ear protection and the controls to the stereo system. When Cannon had wanted to upgrade the whole complex with a speaker system, he hadn't been on board until Cannon spoke through the benefits. Playing the song from when they were in high school hadn't been on Cannon's list, but War was using it for it tonight.

Remington waited on him to get his ear protection on before she turned and tried out her gun. He couldn't find anything in her stance to correct but he wasn't surprised. Remington was driven to be the best at her job and protect those she loved. She paused after she ran through a box and had decimated the target. He replaced the target when it returned and sent it back. He motioned for her to continue. She leaned up and bussed his lips. Her muffled thank you pleased him. He owed Winnie. She'd seemed the most receptive in the texting so once he'd had an idea, he'd texted just her with what he planned. She'd been the one to suggest he should do things

Remington liked to do. Her reasoning had been it would relax Remington and he was grateful. She'd been right.

Remington finished the box, cleared her gun, and laid it on the counter.

"Thank you."

He grinned at how happy she sounded.

"You're welcome. How about we move on to our next portion?"

"There's more?"

He clicked the sound system, leading her out into the open lounge area of the range. She cocked her head at the first notes of the song. Her sisters and she had gone to see it at the theater three times that week because of how much Beth loved the show. His mom had forced him, Bear and Matt to go with them once because she'd been worried about the girls driving by themselves to Dodge City.

"I remember this song playing at prom watching you dancing with your date. Even though at that time I thought you were too high maintenance, I wanted to be him. You were smiling and laughing while you danced. I left right after graduation and lived my life. I don't regret the path I took because I had a lot of growing up to do. What I learned in the Army and later as a police officer helped me become a man. Coming back here, I planned on taking over the MC and living my life. I'd given up thinking I'd find someone to spend the rest of my life with." He paused as Remington stiffened in his arms. "Now, I'm not saying that's where we're at. Heck, I think this is only the second time we've hung out that we haven't fought or had someone get hurt. What I am saying is I want to see where this goes...if you're willing?"

He tried to present a calm façade as he waited for Remington to consider his words, but his palms had started sweating. He'd lied. He could see this ending in marriage, but he'd been such an ass he'd take it slow. He was in his forties but waiting for her reply had him teetering on the edge of a cliff. Would she open herself up?

"Everything you've done tonight has shown me a different side of you. A side I like and want to spend more time with. I think we're right where we're supposed to be. We've both grown over the years and who knows, if we would have tried something years ago, the odds probably would have been against us."

He spun her around as one song segued into the next. He closed his eyes, swaying with her to the music. She relaxed into him, her face resting against his beard. Four months ago, he'd never have imagined he'd be here, with her, and know he was truly home. He didn't remember adding this song to his playlist, but the words were perfect. Her strength, her character was perfect, as if she'd been made for him. They both had their own baggage but when he dreamed of the future, he could see them together. Sure, they'd disagree, raise their voices. They were both passionate about what they believed in. He wasn't one who wanted a woman to submit to him. He craved a partner—someone who would challenge him to be a better man. Remi would do that.

Lips caressing his neck as they traveled up to his ear had him wondering how he was supposed to wait to have her until their third date. With all the blood rushing to his groin, he couldn't remember which sister had given him that directive, but they'd all agreed how important it was.

Remi's lips claimed his, pushing into his mouth, her tongue taking control of their kiss. He grasped her butt, shifting her closer, which wasn't enough. Her arms wrapped around his shoulders, and he hoisted her up as her legs wrapped around his hips. He fumbled toward the counter, setting her there so he could cup her breast. A little moan broke free.

"Not sure what you have planned next but if it involves you inside me, I'm on board," she whispered as she kissed along his jaw.

He wanted her more than he needed his next breath, but he wasn't screwing this up. "I want nothing more but it's not the third date."

Her kisses stopped as she leaned back. "Third date?"

"Your sisters said you wanted a gentleman and that meant no sex until after the third date. They all said it's what you'd want."

"All of them?" she growled.

He rubbed his groin against her mound, watching her eyes dilate. He didn't want to get off track because she was irritated with her sisters. They had all obviously been screwing with him. Dealing with them could wait until later. Right now, he wanted to feel Remi against him. He slid her leather jacket off her and had his hand under her shirt, gliding up to her breast.

"Let's leave getting back at them to later. How about you tell me how you want this date to go? We can leave here and go on a ride, or we can go check out the course."

"Option three," she muttered as she pulled her shirt off and tossed it on the counter.

"Option three?"

Remi had his cut off and laid on her shirt and was tugging his t-shirt over his head.

"Yes. You inside me until we both can't speak."

Her hands had his belt unbuckled and his jeans pushed down to his thighs. Her fingers grasped his cock, running across his piercing. He might have to thank his brother for his prank because it felt wonderful with Remi's touch. He wasn't sure why he'd fought this for so long, but he was fucking glad he'd come to his senses.

He slid closer, unhooking her bra so he could taste her. Her hardened nipples begged for his lips. He smiled at Remi's moan, tugging on her other nipple as he feasted on the one. He didn't want to neglect any part of her. She was tugging her jeans lower as he moved lower and licked along her stomach, playing with her piercing.

"Help me," she pleaded.

He'd give in because he couldn't wait to see her naked, feel her naked and wrapped around him. His hands made quick work of her jeans and panties, laying them on the counter. Remi reached into the pocket, grabbing a condom. He was thankful she was still thinking about consequences because all he cared about was being balls deep in her. This time would have to be fast, but he wasn't fucking her if she wasn't ready. He ran his finger around her clit and then circled her entrance. She was drenched and oh so ready for him. Her fingers had him wrapped and at her entrance.

He paused because he wanted to be sure. "Remi, if we do this, there's no going back. I don't want to be fuck buddies or friends with benefits. I want to build something with you. You'll be mine and only mine as we see where this goes."

Her nod as she moved against him had the tip sliding in. "I need the words, Remi."

"I love it when you call me Remi, but I'll love it more when you get inside me and make me yours."

Thank fuck because he couldn't last a minute longer without being inside her. He thrust in and wished there wasn't anything between them. The possessiveness thrumming inside him surprised him but with Remi, he'd found his one. He tried thinking about anything but how she felt because he didn't think he could handle her remembering their first time as anything less than memorable. Her nails scraped his back.

"I won't break. Harder. I'm so close," she whimpered as she undulated against him.

A couple deep thrusts and she was shaking against him, her pussy clamping down on him. He let the tingle in his back take over, thrusting deep and releasing. He leaned his forehead against hers, trying to catch his breath. He considered himself a strong man. A man capable of locking down his emotions and doing what needed to be done but with Remi, she'd ripped his heart wide open, and every emotion was bubbling to the surface. He wanted to spill everything he was feeling. He held back. His Remi wasn't ready for all the hearts and flowers. He'd opened a chink in her armor, and it was a start. He'd bide his time and let her get used to their new normal before he overwhelmed her with anything else.

Remi cuddled close to War as he took the curve close to her house. She was thankful he wasn't filling her ear with senseless chatter. Even with the ability to chat between their helmets, he was quiet, allowing her to think. It was something she liked about War. He didn't need to fill the silence. He was comfortable in his own skin.

Tonight, she craved the silence because her emotions were all over the place. Having War inside her, arms wrapped around her holding her close, had changed things. She'd known what she was doing. His insistence on her articulating what she wanted had shouted it from the rooftops. He wanted to build a relationship.

Deep down where she didn't want to admit, he was the man she wanted with all his faults, failures and virtues. The question was, could he accept her as she was? She wasn't perfect and had her own faults and failures.

She couldn't stand mess. She needed order. A shrink would probably say it was something to do with the trauma of losing her mom and feeling out of control. It didn't matter to her what caused it, but she was calmer and relaxed when her space was in order.

Of course, it was also what made her good at planning. She'd enjoyed having Bear around because they both thought through what could happen and how to counteract it.

Love, if that was what she was feeling for War, wasn't controllable, wasn't measurable. It flowed and permeated every aspect of life. When her parents were alive, she could feel the love when she walked in a room. It was the same with Regina and Baron. She wasn't sure she was ready for it. At the heart of it, love demanded trust. Trust the other person would have her best interests at heart. Would War be the safe place where she could open up or would he demand to control how she did her job? Could he be okay with the risks her job entailed?

He'd hurt her before. Sure, he'd been in high school, and she'd made mistakes back then, too. Her heart pounded at the thought of what his betrayal would do to her. She trusted those she loved but they were few. Her sisters, her dad, the original MC members, Regina, and then there was the next layer. She had a couple of their employees she'd classified as friends but besides her sisters, she kept her circle small.

She had dreams of a partner who she would grow old with and kids. She even considered adopting by herself, but the hurdles were so large for a single person. She wanted a family. Kids running around and laughter and love filling her home.

War slowed and then backed the motorcycle into the spot. He held out his hand to help her off. She wasn't sure whether she wanted him to come in or leave. Her emotions were bubbling to the surface. She wasn't sure she was ready to share with him yet. He shut the motorcycle off, then took off his helmet, laid it on the seat and gazed into her eyes. She could stare at him forever.

He stepped closer. He smelled of leather, gasoline and the outdoors. Why on him did it smell so good? He grasped her hand, leading her up the steps to her porch. His silence this time was unnerving. He paused and tugged her flush against him. His finger touched her chin and tilted her up to look in his eyes.

"Tonight, with you, Remi, was more than I imagined. I can't think of anything I want more than to walk in your house and spend the rest of the night showing you how much you mean to me. I also know you're someone who considers all the angles and might need some time to think. I have a six am meeting in Bluff Creek I can't miss. Baron, Regina, and I are meeting at the diner, but I'll do whatever you want. It's your choice."

She was torn. Having him in her bed and waking up with him sounded wonderful but he was right. A lot had changed tonight. She was a planner. Someone who considered all the scenarios, and his early morning meeting gave her the excuse to have a little time to think.

"I loved everything about tonight. It was perfect, but I do need some time to think. So, how about you kiss me goodnight?"

She'd come to love seeing his lips stretch in a grin. His finger caressed down her cheek.

"That I can do."

His lips claimed hers, having her regretting her decision to send him away tonight. Heat pooled and had her pressing her mound against him. He pulled away, chuckling.

"You are too much of a temptation. If you don't get inside, I'll forget I gave you a choice."

War's possessive words thrilled her even though she'd known he'd never do anything she didn't consent to. His protective nature wouldn't allow him to. She unlocked the door and stood in the doorway, gazing at the man she'd spent her lifetime wanting. It was hard to believe he was in front of her, and he craved her. He motioned her to shut and lock the door. She nodded and closed the door, locking it and leaning back against it. War's steps echoed off the porch then his motorcycle rumbled. She was sure she'd replay the whole date and overthink every word and action but for now, she was enjoying how he made her feel treasured.

She didn't turn on the lights as she walked through her house. For now, she didn't want to share any part of War with her sisters. If they saw the lights on, they'd come to visit. If not, they'd leave her alone until morning. She'd have a little reprieve before deciding what she'd share, if anything. Before she'd had no problem sharing it all but tonight was different.

Chapter Eighteen

Remington finished wiping down the area. It was the next to last item on the list Winnie had handed her when she'd arrived. Completing the tasks had given her plenty of time to reflect on the last month dating War. They'd spent a lot of time together growing and learning about each other. He'd learned her obsessively neat habits and had made sure he abided by her rules after she'd washed all his white t-shirts he'd dropped by the bed with a new pair of red panties she'd bought. When he had to wear a pink t-shirt to his meeting, he'd promised to pick up after himself.

She'd learned although he saw her as a fully capable woman, when they were together, he wanted to pay, open doors for her and always walked closest to the street. She might bitch and moan at him but secretly she was pleased. His protectiveness didn't diminish her abilities. It let her know he cherished her. When he'd accompanied her on a skip because he wanted to know more about her job, he'd stepped back and followed her directions.

They hadn't had a security job together. After they'd added another layer of questions and done a deep dive, three jobs had cancelled in the last two months. They'd been overwhelmed before, so she'd considered it a blessing. She'd been able to push off any of the interviews she'd been contemplating. Sarah and Scoop were still following trails but besides linking one of their survivor clients to him, it had been a dead end.

Once War got back in town, they planned on another group meeting with all the MC members and her and her sisters. They had to be missing something.

They'd had multiple meetings, and everyone was getting frustrated. She'd missed War this week. He and some of the guys had gone to visit their Texas chapter. He hadn't said much beyond they were needed. She and War had found their way during dating about what she wanted to know and what he was willing to share. If she and War moved further along, they'd be having a conversation. She wasn't willing to not have a hundred percent honesty. She wasn't going to be happy with 'it's club business' and go on her way. If it could affect her or her family, she'd rather know than be blindsided.

He'd texted hours ago when they headed back. He'd thought they'd be back before the first fight tonight. Roam had gone, too, so she'd been helping Regina with his kids. They'd had a sleepover at her house earlier in the week. With all three of them, she'd given in and requested her sisters as reinforcements. Her dad had noticed everyone showing up and come over, too. He'd cuddled Georgia in a rocking chair for hours. He'd mentioned at least twice when they were all in the room together how good he looked holding her and how happy he'd be when he had grandkids of his own. It had been a complete turnaround from him telling them to be careful.

She wanted kids and lately, she'd been daydreaming of War being their dad. Whether they were boys or girls, she didn't care. She wanted kids. She only hoped her body didn't try to say it was too late. She wasn't averse to adopting but the idea of being pregnant was growing on her. War was wonderful with his niece and nephews. Kind, loving but firm when Grant was being ornery. She'd even started thinking through how the business could run efficiently if and when she was pregnant. Which had led to thinking about the other jobs and how to cover them if her sisters were pregnant. God help them all if they were pregnant at the same time. Though having kids close together would be nice.

She glanced around the gym. Everything looked ready but she hadn't seen Winnie for a while. Normally Winnie would have flitted through doublechecking everything. She was the perfect person for the gym because she loved finding what worked for people. Her passion for helping people become healthy and maintain with a personalized program was a joy to watch.

Remi had to admit, though, when Winnie focused on the less than healthy snacks in her cabinets, she considered changing the locks on her house. It came from a good place but when all the snacks in her cabinets had been removed and replaced with fruit in the refrigerator, they'd had to come to an agreement. Remington would work on eating healthier as long as Winnie left her emergency snacks alone. Winnie's worry was understandable. She'd grieved longer losing their mom and it had fueled her passion for health. Even though a healthier lifestyle wouldn't have kept their mom from getting breast cancer.

Remington walked back toward the office then paused. A shiver worked up her spine. Something felt off and she never ignored her instincts. She'd already changed into gym clothes. Her gun was locked inside her locker. Although they had a couple of special places in the gym where a spare was concealed, they weren't close to where she was.

She walked slowly toward the office. She'd check the cameras and see if anything was off. She grabbed the mop near the office, unscrewing the handle from the mop end. It was better than nothing and Winnie could laugh at her when she walked in, and everything would be great. The door to the office was partially open but she couldn't see in. Stepping closer, she paused, listening. Nothing out of the ordinary. She pushed open the door, walking around to the monitors. Her heart pounded as she rushed to Winnie, lying on the floor, blood spreading out from her head. She checked her pulse, then glanced toward the monitors as something flittered in the corner of her eye and pain exploded from her head. A second blow across her shoulders had her dropping down. She fought to keep her eyes open, but everything darkened.

Chapter Nineteen

War couldn't wait to see Remington. He'd never thought he'd be one of those men who couldn't get a woman out of his head, but he'd changed. Remi wasn't only in his head, she was in his heart. A week away had convinced him that she was it for him. He'd been biding his time, but he wasn't waiting any longer. Remington was his. He'd ordered her a property cut and was having one of his altered. His heart was owned by her. She was strong and could handle anything, but her softer side would make her a wonderful mom to their kids. And oh, they were having kids. He couldn't wait to see her pregnant. She'd mentioned once how she wanted kids but wasn't sure she'd be able to. He'd never realized the pressure women felt as they aged. Whether she was able to carry their kids, or they adopted, they'd have a family. Holding her in bed, reassuring her whatever their road was, he'd be there had felt like a turning point for them. Her shoulders had relaxed.

Bear hadn't gone down to Texas with them, so he'd tasked him with fulfilling one of his goals for Remington. Hopefully his task in Dodge City had gone well. He'd authorized him to do whatever it took to allow the girls back in the bar they were banned from. Of course, he'd also offered the incentive of being the only bar in Kansas to serve Bluff Creek Brotherhood's brew. Their Texas chapter had been growing that part of their business and War wasn't above using anything at his disposal to make one of Remi's dreams come true.

They'd crossed over into Kansas and were only about thirty minutes out. Bear had said he'd meet them there and would arrive about the same time if traffic wasn't bad from Dodge City. As they crested the next hill, smoke covered the sky on the horizon. The last month had been dry, and they'd been under a burn ban. Hopefully, someone hadn't decided to ignore it. Winds were normal today, around fifteen miles an hour, which was plenty to spread a wildfire.

He'd told Remi he'd be there by the first fight. He loved watching her show off her skills. The way her muscles moved underneath her skin always had him adjusting himself. Everything she did turned him on and had him wanting to be alone with her.

Although smoke on the horizon could look closer than it really was, he was getting worried. If it was a wildfire, the color would have stayed white, but it was turning darker and still building. He had that feeling in the pit of his stomach of something wrong. That feeling had saved him multiple times in the Army and later as an officer. He'd only ignored it once, but he couldn't think about that. His phone rang and he hit his watch to answer. His Bluetooth headset had been great on the trip.

"Yes?"

He didn't recognize the number.

"Code Ross at gym. Medical and fire notified. Repeat Code Ross. This message is a recording."

He floored it until he was pushing his motorcycle as fast as it could go. He had questions and no answers. The fire on the horizon had to be the gym. Was Remi or anyone in there when it caught fire? Who was hurt if they were notifying medical? Maybe everyone was fine, and they were being careful, but he didn't think so. As far as they were from fire and medical, it could have been done as a precaution.

The last ten miles seemed to stretch. Minutes he spent imagining worst-case scenarios. The biggest question—was Remi already there? He hoped and prayed not. He'd grown up going to church with his mom and dad but hadn't been in years. He believed in God but had been disillusioned with how good people died and the scum of the earth who hurt the innocent seemed to flourish. But now, he prayed because he couldn't lose Remi.

"Call Remi," he directed. The phone rang then went to voicemail.

She'd become a part of the fabric of his life so deeply woven in, being in Texas had been agony. He wasn't sure how he'd deal with them being apart for weeks at a time when she had a job, but he'd deal. What he couldn't deal with was losing her forever.

He tried one more time as he and the others took the turn onto the gym road with the same response—no answer. Multiple vehicles were parked near the gym and his worst fears were realized. The structure was engulfed. He set the kickstand, took off his helmet and ran toward the structure. The owner of the diner was standing by his truck, watching the flames with his arm around one of kids he recognized from his first night here.

"What happened?"

"I came to drop off the food and noticed the smoke as I turned onto the road. I thought some fool was ignoring the burn ban. When I got here, it was engulfed. I called the bail bonds company. Nobody answered. It continued to ring. I called 911 then tried each of the girls' cell phones. No one is answering. The doors were blocked from the outside. I moved stuff and tried to go in, but the flames were too high."

He took off running. The only reason doors would be blocked was if someone was inside. As he got closer, the heat took his breath away. How could his Remi survive this heat and smoke?

Hands grabbed him and pulled him back. He turned to see who dared keep him away from Remi.

"Hold up, I've got the camera. We should be able to see if anyone's in there." Cannon waved the thermal imaging camera they'd ordered for the tactical course and brought back with them from Texas.

War watched the screen as they walked around the building toward the office. He could see the heat from different parts of the building and even pieces of the ceiling on fire falling but no bodies. Two parts of the building had caved in. He wasn't a fire investigator, but it was suspicious with what he knew about the building and their fire suppression system. Noah and his daughters would never have done anything unsafe.

"There's no one inside."

If she wasn't inside, where was she and why were none of her sisters answering the phone? The automated message seemed like a last-ditch effort. The two prospects who'd come back with them from Texas ran over.

"I checked the well to see if we could get a hose going. Someone cut the lines to the pump."

The screech of a siren filled the air along with the roar of pipes. Bear pulled in right before the ambulance and ran over.

"Where's Winnie and Remington?"

He shook his head. "We can't find anyone."

"Did you check the hatch?"

"What hatch?"

Bear didn't answer but took off running across the field, hopping the barbed-wire fence. War followed with Cannon. Bear had a head start and he'd always been fast. Bear paused at something on the ground, pulling his gun.

War pulled his and stopped. Bear had yanked off the cap on the guy's head. His shoulder was bleeding along with his ankle. He screeched as Bear pressed his boot on the ankle wound.

"Where are they?"

"I don't know and I'm not talking without a lawyer."

Bear chuckled. "Do you think I look like the person who is going to call a lawyer for you? Who shot you?"

"That bitch. I came out to make sure no one escaped. She came out of the lean-to and shot me."

"Cannon, tie him up and we'll talk with him later. War, come with me."

War could care less his VP was giving him orders. Once he'd realized Remington could be in the structure, he couldn't think straight. He kept wondering if his ineptitude had killed another woman. The attacker had called it a lean-to, but it wasn't like any lean-to he'd seen. It had three full sides with the fourth having a four-foot-wide opening. The floor was cement when he'd only seen them as dirt. He followed Bear in. Bear stepped around a four-foot cement wall blocking the back third of the structure. He leaned down, swept some straw away and did something that beeped.

"Come on."

Bear opened a hatch and turned to go down a metal ladder. War followed him, closing the hatch and twisting it to lock it. He joined Bear at what looked like a crossroads. One tunnel led to the right, and another led to the left which would be back toward the gym. He'd grabbed a flashlight and a walkie-talkie from a shelf. Flipping it on, he waited.

"This is Bear. Code Chandler. I say again. Code Chandler. Holding at Crossroad."

He took a deep breath, waiting to see if anyone would reply. He'd learned their codes but for the life of him, he couldn't remember what Code Chandler was. Remi was missing. He'd known she was coming to mean a lot to him, and he was in love, but the thought of never having her again had him wanting to drop to his knees.

"Code Joey. Evac site homestead."

He might not remember Chandler, but he'd heard Code Joey when Bear was injured. Someone was hurt. He had a hard time catching his breath imagining it was his Remi. Bear grabbed his arm, pulling him to a golf cart, pushing him into the passenger seat. Bear started it and floored it to the homestead. Jesse must have gotten her hands on it and modified it because they were going faster than he'd ever had a golf cart go but it was still too slow for him. Bear parked it by another golf cart and he followed him to another ladder on the wall.

"Code Chandler. Entering homestead."

Bear didn't wait for a reply, just punched in the code and was up the ladder, opening the hatch. War followed as quickly as he could. What he saw had him pausing. They were in what looked like a safe room but was larger than any he'd ever seen.

One wall held medical supplies and had two beds. Remi and Winnie were each sitting on one while Jesse was holding oxygen to Remi's face. Winnie's arm was haphazardly bandaged as if she'd taken care of herself. Sarah was monitoring one wall of computers along with Beth. Locks had the door to the outside room open and had a gun in his hand in addition to the rifle over his shoulder and a bulletproof vest on his chest.

He ran over to Remi, pulling her close. "I don't know how you got out and I don't care. I only care I can have you in my arms. I've never been so scared in my life."

Remi leaned into him, coughing behind the mask. Bear was standing by Winnie, trying to check on her but she batted his hand away.

"Ambulance is here. Everyone is going to get checked out, no exceptions, but I want security," Noah directed. "Jesse, what have you got?"

"I finished the upgrade on the first SUV. I could drive separately with War and Bear while Remi and Winnie go in the ambulance. You, Sarah and Beth along with some of the MC could stay here. This was a coordinated attack. If I'd planned it, the burning of the gym would be wave one to get everyone distracted before I hit with wave two. Everyone needs to be on alert." Jesse's no-nonsense voice gave him a sense of control for the first time since he'd spotted the smoke. At least she was thinking critically.

Locks nodded as Flick came in with a stretcher along with his partner. War was surprised Locks was letting his partner into what he'd term a safe room but maybe Noah trusted him.

Flick's eyes glanced around the room, cataloguing injuries. His shoulders relaxed after his survey.

"It looks like we can all go get checked out at the hospital."

War relaxed a little. Even though he'd seen Remi with his own eyes and held her in his arms, he'd still been concerned. The closest hospital was thirty minutes away and wasn't equipped for anything major. After today, he'd be adding a full clinic on his wish list for the MC. He might need to recruit some more members with specific skill sets. He was grateful Remington or Winchester weren't hurt worse but if they had been, he couldn't imagine someone having to wait an hour to be transported to a major hospital.

Winchester stood up and Bear immediately grabbed her arm.

"I'm not going to fall but I wanted to thank you. Your worst-case scenario thinking which had us adding the hatch in the office is what saved us. If only we'd used you to help us on adding new security people."

"Explain," Bear growled.

"Don't use that tone with me when my head is hurting. A new guy who was wearing one of our security shirts hit me over the head and knocked me out. I may be all sunshine and roses but I have no problem kicking you into next week when you piss me off."

Bear's eyes blazed and War could see this deteriorating. If they were going to get Remington and Winnie checked out, he needed to calm this down, though he was close to exploding.

Remington pulled her oxygen mask off so she could speak. "Winnie, we haven't hired any new people in security in the last thirty days. You've met all of them."

Remington's raspy voice worried him but someone who had gotten on the property with a security company shirt worried him more.

"This guy said Dad sent him and asked to help. When I turned to show him the boxes to move, something hit the back of my neck and head, and it was lights out. Luckily, the hot embers hitting my hands woke me up otherwise the hatch wouldn't have mattered."

He needed to have the women checked out and then they'd need answers to how someone was able to get past the security.

"Get my daughters checked out then we'll meet here for pancakes."

Did he honestly hear Locks right? Multiple people had attacked them. The gym was burnt to the ground, he had an assailant to chat with, and Locks wanted fucking pancakes. Just as he started to blast Locks, Remington's hand on his arm stopped him.

"Dad, explain before War goes ballistic."

Remi's words had a small grin quirking the side of his mouth as he nodded.

"Pancakes were Kathryn's code for solving any problems. We'd meet in the kitchen with pancakes, bacon and whatever else she came up with and work through any issue. It stuck and we use it now."

He ran his hand down Remi's arm, reminding himself he didn't lose her today. He could honor their traditions even though his first inclination was to lock Remington in the safe room and never let her out. His head was screaming she and Winnie had rescued themselves, but his heart was yelling at him to protect his warrior woman at any cost.

"You heard the man. Let's get checked out then Code Pancakes."

Chapter Twenty

Remington sipped her hot tea while waiting for a break in the conversation. She and Winnie had been checked out. They'd both been hit on the head, but the doctor had been fine with releasing them as long as someone was watching them. Flick was still on duty, but he and his partner were eating pancakes with them. If called, they'd respond, otherwise they were good to stay at the house.

War's leg was vibrating under her hand. He wasn't used to not being in charge. She admired his restraint in allowing her dad to lead the conversation. Every so often, he'd shove another piece of pancake in his mouth and chew. As yet, he hadn't commented, just listened.

She'd directed Sarah to record the conversation. Her head was aching enough she was concerned she'd miss something. Her instincts were shouting that how could the shooting and the attack not be related but she'd learned never to discount any option.

Winnie hadn't said much. Bear was trying, in his own way, to take care of her and if it didn't hurt to smile, she'd be grinning at their behavior.

"Remington, thoughts?"

It was just like her dad calling on her for her opinion when she wasn't really listening, but she'd dealt with him for years.

"I think everyone has great points and guesses but we don't know anything. I vote we all stay here at the main house tonight. Three from security can roam outside and we'll have one on the monitors inside, trading out with a relief shift in three hours. The gym will have the fire crews there the rest of the night. I'm not in charge of the MC but I feel like we can't discount that whoever did this was gunning for all of us."

War nodded, patting her thigh. "I agree. Baron has the MC on lockdown. With it being the weekend, we're not going to allow anyone on the property who isn't affiliated with us. The orchard wasn't open this weekend and the gun range is going to have a plumbing issue which requires closure. The garage will be open but isn't going to accept any new customers. They have some jobs that have to be finished."

"We've got a plan. We're Code Burke."

Remi stood and tugged War's hand to follow her. Tonight wasn't how she planned on being in bed with War. He'd been gone and she'd spent entirely too much time imagining all the ways she could have him in her bed, on the couch and in the shower. Her head hurt with each step she took so her plans would have to wait. She grabbed a key from the kitchen wall. Her dad had remodeled the main house once they'd moved out. Each bedroom now had its own full bathroom, small kitchen area with a microwave and mini refrigerator along with a king-sized bed and a couple recliners. The doors were steel, and the key locked the deadbolt. He'd made each room as close to impenetrable as possible.

She wasn't sure she had enough strength to shower but didn't want to have her dirty body on the sheets.

"Sit here." War led her to the toilet. He turned the shower on then turned to her and paused. "I want to help you take your clothes off, but I'm worried I'll hurt your head."

Remi raised her arms up in reply. War showering her was the only way it was going to happen. He quickly had her undressed and himself. He lifted her up, stepping into the shower, letting the hot water hit her shoulders while keeping the spray away from her bandage.

"You just relax and let me help you."

His lips kissed her forehead. "I was so fucking scared, Rem. Having you in my arms, I can finally breathe."

His words had her ready to cry but she hated crying. It only gave her a headache.

"When I woke up with Winnie shaking my shoulder and coughing with the flames around us, all I could think of was getting us out so I could see you. There's so much I haven't said but I knew if I could just get to you and have your arms around me then everything would be okay."

War sat her on the shower seat and knelt in front of her, his eyes cataloguing each scrape and bruise. Her hand had been slick with blood when they went through the hatch and down the ladder. She'd lost her grip and scraped her palms trying to catch herself.

"Rem, you amaze me. You're strong, sexy, a fighter, and I want to wrap you in cotton wool to keep you from ever having any scrapes, but then you wouldn't be you. Instead, I want you to know, my arms will always be a safe place where you don't have to be strong. I won't think less of you when you need someone to lean on and will never judge you for crying. I'll protect you until you're ready to fight again."

He squirted body soap on a cloth and ran it over her, cleaning each scrape. His hands were loving though it wasn't sexual. It was a man caring for his woman. As she'd aged, she'd given up on finding a man who could handle her strength and her job. War's love didn't diminish her strength, it increased it because she knew no matter what he'd be there for her. War finished, turned the shower off and reached for a towel, while keeping a hand on her. She was grateful because she wasn't sure how much longer she could stay upright. He wrapped the towel around her and lifted her in his arms.

"T-shirt or naked?"

He set her on the end of the bed and used another towel to pat her legs dry while he waited for her answer.

"T-shirt. Just in case there's a second wave."

"Okay. You good? I'm going to grab shirts and shorts for us along with some antibiotic ointment to reapply to your scrapes."

She nodded. It would take every ounce of strength she possessed to stay upright but if she could last a little longer, she could cuddle up with War and let him watch over her. When Winnie had shaken her awake, her first deep breath of the smoke had her coughing. For a second, she couldn't think of what to do next. She'd allowed the fear to override everything she knew. Winnie had screamed her name, pulled her up and directed her actions. She was always in charge and if Winnie hadn't been there, she wasn't sure what would have happened to her. She'd come so close to losing today.

She'd been scared when she and Bear were under fire, but she trained for those type of scenarios. Nothing had prepared her for being surrounded by fire, the smoke so thick she couldn't breathe. Bear's thinking and her dad's insistence that they hook the gym to the underground tunnels had saved them. When she could think clearly, she'd be looking at what they could do to make everywhere safer. Tonight, she wanted to close her eyes and be held in War's arms.

"Remi, baby, it's okay."

War tilted her head up, wiping the tears away. His arms slid around her gently. He was being so careful not to touch where she was hurt. He bent to let her forehead lean on his shoulders, tugging her close, patting her back. She was so tired of always being strong. With War, she could let him shoulder the load. They were a team and she'd never been more grateful for it than tonight.

His scent fresh from the shower was a comfort. It was home for her. Until he'd come home, she hadn't realized how much was missing. He'd found that part of her hidden away, burrowed his way in and filled it with his love. His love made her more. He didn't expect her to change. In fact, he supported her so she could fly as high as possible but was there to soothe her when she was at her lowest.

With him, she could be herself. She'd dreamed of having the type of relationship her mom and dad had. Their love and Baron and Regina's had set the bar high, but she'd found it.

"Let it all out, then we can sleep. You were so fucking strong getting out of there. I'll always be your safe place."

Remi relaxed as War's lips brushed her forehead and closed her eyes. War would take care of everything. She could worry about the attack tomorrow.

War held Remi, patting her back until her muscles relaxed. He maneuvered her around, sliding her shirt on, then her panties and shorts. Tucking her on her side with a pillow supporting her until he could lie beside her, he grabbed his and Remi's shoes and their guns, setting them close by. Cleaning his hands, he checked the room before crawling in beside her, then wrapped his arms around her, situating her head on his shoulder. He doubted he'd sleep deeply, and he wanted to ensure she didn't roll to her back. Having her bandage hit the pillow would wake her up. He set his alarm for her next dose of pain pills.

He took his first deep breath since he'd seen the fire. Even after he'd known Remi was alive, he'd still had a weight on his chest worrying about her. He fought down his inclination to keep her locked away and protect her from everything but that wasn't the woman he'd fallen in love with. He'd fallen for a woman who was a warrior. He understood what his dad had been telling him. Remi didn't need him standing in front of her. She required a partner, a king to her queen. She might not be his princess, but she was certainly his queen. The woman he would fight beside to ensure she had all her dreams.

Imagining his warrior woman as a mom had him worried for anyone who threatened her kids. He'd pushed the thought of having children away while he was gone. No one had ever made him imagine children in his future but with Remington, everything was possible.

He'd worried when he and Remi started dating how he would handle her and her job, but this situation was different. Remington strategized and took calculated risks. She didn't run into places and take stupid chances. His concern and anxiety over her job wasn't based on her. It had been based on his history, which was *his* problem. He'd kept his past from

Remi because he'd assumed she'd find him lacking but she wouldn't. She'd probably call him a dumbass for not recognizing the fault was his rookie's, not his. Sometimes people made choices and those left had to deal with the fallout. Until he was back in Bluff Creek, he hadn't dealt with it. He'd pushed it down deep, but let it affect every decision he'd made.

He had a lot to share with his woman and it was time he did. She deserved the best version of him, and he was going to make sure she got it.

Noah's freaking tunnels had been a lifesaver. He'd need to find out how they came about and how long they took. He could see them being something he wanted added to the MC compound. He had a huge to-do list starting with chatting with Jesse about what she was doing to the bail bonds' SUVs and see if they needed a couple of vehicles modified. All of their businesses were legitimate, but it didn't preclude them from getting attacked.

A man with a security company shirt was unnerving. Where did he come from and how did he get it? With an undetermined threat, he wanted something which had pictures of all the bail bonds and security people so he could memorize them. He also wanted Remi and her sisters to be familiar with everyone in any way connected to the MC to protect them from having this happen again.

For now, he was going to hold his woman and get a little sleep. Tomorrow he'd worry about all the crazy codes his woman and her sisters had and how they could protect their families.

Chapter Twenty-one

War finished his coffee before heading into the main room. It'd been two weeks since he'd come so close to losing everything but thank goodness, he hadn't. Although everyone was working on the issue, they had no idea who had planned the attack.

The fire inspector had determined four bombs strapped to the main support pillars had brought down the gym. Unfortunately, Bear's worst-case scenarios had never considered bombs at the gym. Sarah was beside herself trying to determine how someone had been able to circumvent their systems to get in the gym, plant the bombs and leave no trace of who they were. Video footage had shown a dark gym. Scoop had reviewed everything, but he'd been stumped, too.

They were on a modified lockdown in that they weren't allowing anyone not living at the compound past the first set of gates. They'd spent a day and half digging holes and putting in new steel posts and large gates to separate the orchard and farm from the houses on the compound.

Roam and Rascal had reported a couple more incidents of things being off at the tattoo shop and Scoop had ordered the equipment and would install it as soon as it came in.

Remi had planned a night with her sisters tonight. It was the first time in the last two weeks he wouldn't be sleeping by her. He was going to use the time to check on his brothers. The stress of the last two weeks was taking its toll.

As he pushed the door open into the main room, a stench worse than anything he'd smelled on the force assaulted his nostrils. Baron, Rascal and Locks were playing cards. Casper and Georgia were playing on the floor beside them.

"What the hell is that smell and why haven't you fixed it?"

Baron chuckled and hi-fived Noah. "Son, that is your niece and she's ready for you to change her diaper."

"Why the heck would I have to change her diaper? Aren't you guys in charge of her?"

"Yes, but she tried new vegetables yesterday. Her body is not liking them. We've each changed her once already."

"What does that have to do with that smell?" He shook his head because he knew this wasn't going to end well for him.

"As long as she wasn't unhappy, we were ignoring it. Whoever mentioned it first had to change her. Winner, winner, War."

He wanted to smack the smile off his father's face, but he wasn't letting sweet little Georgia sit in her smelly poop. The whole room reeked. He shook his head and walked over, picking up his niece.

"I don't know what vegetables they gave you, kid, but you should stay away from them."

Taking her in the nursery his mom had added to the clubhouse, he popped the snaps on her onesie. Tugging it up, he blinked his eyes as they started to water.

"Man, Georgia, we've got to get you smelling better. Little girls should be sunshine and roses. Right now, you smell like you rolled in cow poop."

He tugged his t-shirt above his nose to try to stem the smell. Pulling the tabs on her diaper, he almost yelled for his mom. Yellow-orange poop wasn't only on her butt. It had filled the diaper. He gagged a little and grabbed the wipes.

"I love you, Georgie girl, but we're getting you on a better diet."

She smiled at him as he cleaned her up. Despite how bad she smelled, he could see a little girl just like her only with Remington's beautiful brown eyes. Georgia's little hand smacked his arm as he finished the diaper.

"Yep, sweetie pie. I think Remi and I need to make sure you have some cousins to play with."

He grabbed another outfit. As bad as she smelled, he couldn't imagine her outfit didn't stink, too. He pulled a cute outfit with ruffles on the butt and wrestled her into it. Every time he came close to getting her arm through, she moved. When he finished, he put her on the floor while he disposed of the diaper and washed his hands, keeping one eye on her. She was starting to crawl, and he knew how fast she could move.

Picking her up, he walked back out. The room still smelled, and the originals were still playing cards. He almost wondered if the vegetables had bothered Casper, too, but he wasn't saying a word.

Although they weren't changing the diapers, he couldn't think of any better men for his kids to be raised around than Baron, Rascal and Locks.

He'd been all gung-ho after Remington had been hurt to immediately get her a property cut and propose but the further out from the fire, the more he realized it was his fear speaking. Remington was it for him and he wasn't cheating her out of anything, including the perfect road to marriage.

The best decision he'd made was coming back to Bluff Creek Brotherhood and his family. He'd found a woman who was more than he could imagine. Now, he had to figure out who wanted to hurt them and how to stop them.

Roam walked in and paused, rearing back at the smell.

"Please tell me that's one of you old guys and not my kid that nuked the room."

Grant walked in with a clothespin on his nose. "Daddy lost. You got to change Casper's poopy diaper. It's really stinking up the room."

War smiled and held his hand out to Grant. "Why don't you and I walk with your sister out to the swing set? It should smell better out there."

Oh yeah, he could totally do this kid thing—poopy diapers and all.

Chapter Twenty-Two

Remi grabbed her tray of beer-battered onion rings and the dips to go along with them before grabbing her keys. It irritated her that she had to lock her door. Although the lockdown was needed, having to deal with locking her door when she was running to Winnie's for the evening was ridiculous. Once they got past this crisis, they all needed to seriously look at upgrading their security procedures and how to keep everyone safe.

Walking over to Winnie's, she noticed Regina's truck and a figure sitting on the front porch. Holding the tray with one hand, she pulled her beretta out, holding it by her side. Keeping armed while on the compound was just another change. She always had one close at hand, but she and her dad had demanded everyone carry. No exceptions.

The figure stayed seated but held up his hands. "It's me, Remington. I'm Regina's protection tonight."

She nodded at one of the prospects from Texas. She recognized him from the pictures Sarah had distributed to them. No one was tricking them again.

She pushed the door open and relaxed her shoulders. Her sisters had their theme song from *Friends* playing. No matter what, she knew her sisters would always be there for her. They and Regina were gathered around Winnie's kitchen island. Big enough to seat eight, she wondered if it would collapse at the amount of food on it. It seemed everyone had the same idea she had about needing comfort food tonight.

She laid down her offering to tonight's festivities and gave Winnie a hug. Then, she hugged each of the women who made life bearable until she got to Regina. She held in her emotions for a second but then let them go. She'd cried a little bit with War, but she'd been shoving each emotion down trying to be the leader they needed her to be.

Regina's arms wrapped around her. One hand patted her shoulder. "It's about time you let loose, girl. I know I've cried more worried about the what ifs this last week than I did when War and Roam were overseas."

She stayed in Regina's arms for a minute, just letting her sisters' conversations drift around her. She'd been scared for herself, but she'd never have forgiven herself if they'd lost Winnie. She pulled away, taking the seat beside Regina.

"Better?" Winnie questioned.

"Yes."

"You know it wasn't your fault," Sarah stated, patting her shoulder.

"Actually, it was her fault you all survived. If she, Dad and Bear hadn't decided to expand the tunnels, we would have lost you both." Jesse's no-nonsense voice and calm face helped remind her she had done something right.

"Now that the crying is done, I want to know about War. Like everything. And if it's parts Regina shouldn't hear, just tell her to cover her ears. Is he everything you dreamed of? Is he pierced? Does he have tattoos hidden under those thigh-hugging jeans?" Beth peppered the questions, not waiting for Remi to answer.

"Yes. Yes, and there's a story there. And yes, but I'm so scared of what's ahead that I don't know how I feel about it."

"Okay, I'm going to have to know the story about the piercing," Sarah requested.

"Well, remember when we lost to Roam, and we let him pierce us?"

Her sisters all nodded. They had all gotten piercings except for Sarah who hadn't played because she had a migraine.

"I knew he was cheating!" Beth yelled.

Remi nodded, watching her sisters all clue in that Roam had cheated.

"I'm not telling you all where War is pierced but I will say the twins had to get intimately acquainted for it to happen."

Regina shook her head, covering her face. "I really wish I would have brought ear plugs for that."

Remi loved these women. They got her and she couldn't imagine life without them, which was why she was torn on how to move forward with War. She couldn't imagine not living this close to her sisters. Intellectually she'd known they would all eventually get married. They all wanted a family, but she'd never considered what it would mean. She imagined them all living close where their kids could go back and forth between houses. How would that work if they all got married and moved away? She wanted to go to sleep beside War and wake up in the morning to his gorgeous blue-grey eyes shining with his love.

"Remi, tell me your best-case scenario with War," Sarah directed.

"We live together forever, having kids and growing old together. I switch to admin more while I'm pregnant if I can get pregnant. If not, we'll adopt. The kids come to work with me at our company daycare if they aren't spending time with family.

We'll all be close by so as you find your one, our kids grow up with their cousins. I don't think I can give up being able to run next door and see you, but War will always need to be on the compound."

She wiped a tear because talking about what she might not be able to have had the tears starting again.

"Oh, Remi. Is that why you've been so quiet this week?" Winnie pulled her close, wrapping an arm around her waist.

She nodded, scrutinizing their faces. Did they think she was crazy to want the world? Did they even want the same thing? None of them had ever mentioned leaving the company and their homes but maybe she'd missed something.

"I might have heard something that could fix it all," Beth stated, then grabbed a slice of pumpkin bread and took a bite.

"You can't just say that then eat. Spill it, sister."

"Tell us."

"Don't keep us waiting."

The sisters' words flew, bringing a smile to Beth's face. She loved knowing a secret.

"I was picking up eggs from Clancey. He told me he'd like to sell his farm, but he wants it to go to someone who could appreciate it and would agree to keep the farmhouse he and his wife built intact. It's definitely more of a hobby farm because he only has a chicken coop for his flock and about ten cows. He'd want the animals to go with the farm."

"How big is his farm?" Regina asked.

"He owns all the land between our two properties and his property goes back and includes the small stream that breaks off from Bluff Creek. It's 3840 acres."

Remi waited to see what her sisters had to say. She wanted this to be a family decision before they took it to the MC and her dad.

"Although I can't guarantee who I'll marry, I have zero plans to live anywhere else. If the man I fall in love with can't see what we have here, then he's not my one."

Sarah's words had Remi relaxing a little. She wanted the dream—the fairy tale but with a badass spin. Where the prince was an MC president, who rode a Harley and didn't rescue the woman—he empowered her.

"It sounds exactly like what we need. Regina, haven't Dad and Baron been wanting to connect the properties?" Jesse questioned.

"Yes. Times have changed and people's views have changed. Plus, Locks said the bail bonds and security are large enough now to withstand losing business if someone doesn't want to work with the MC. I think this is a fantastic idea."

"I worked up a sketch since I've had longer to think about it. Instead of rebuilding the gym where it is, we could use the barn he has and add on to it for the gym. It's close to the road, so we could add a large fence, keeping it a little separate. There'd be a way through to the rest of the property but wouldn't be easily accessible," Beth finished, sliding her sketch in front of them.

Remi had no idea Beth was this talented at drawing, too. She'd rearranged the entrance to the orchard and farm so no one had access to the houses or the clubhouse.

Remi walked around the island, grabbing Beth and spinning her around. "You are the best."

Beth giggled. "I try."

Regina tapped the paper, nodding her head. "This is perfect. When is he putting it on the market? The last thing we want is someone buying it who hates the MC."

"He's waiting for an offer from us. He's holding it because he said he and his farm wouldn't have survived the lean years without the Bluff Creek Brotherhood MC."

"Okay, well we have stuff we need to talk about with the men but right now, I want to hear how all of you ladies are doing. I've been around the clubhouse too much. Catch me up."

Remi listened to her sisters catch up Regina. Winnie sidestepped all questions when Regina brought it around to someone special. Remi had wondered after seeing Winnie at the hospital if she had a thing for Bear but maybe she was mistaken. She hadn't been at her best then.

"I have one more thing I want to show you," Beth said, sliding another piece of paper over to them.

Remi looked at the drawing with wings, a heart, and the words Kathryn's Wings on the ribbon. "Is this a tattoo?"

Beth nodded. "I thought we could all honor Mom and the project she inspired. I'm going to schedule mine this week."

Sarah laughed, pulling out loaf after loaf of pumpkin bread. "Beth showed me the sketch yesterday, so I made enough for everyone to pay," she air quoted, "for their tattoos."

Regina sniffed as tears filled her eyes. "I love it. Your mom would be so proud of all of you. I miss her every day, but I'm blessed you guys let me stand in for her."

Remi cuddled into her sisters and their group hug, thankful they were all together. She'd needed tonight. Sometimes they just hung out and other times they solved each other's problems or helped the person figure out how to solve them on their own. After talking and laughing with her sisters, she felt lighter and ready to take on anything. She'd enjoy tonight and then they needed to schedule a meeting to figure out who was trying to kill them. It was time to take the fight to them.

Chapter Twenty-Three

Remington stopped the SUV, hiding her smile. It had taken everything for War to not say anything about her driving them on their date. Of course, he had no idea that they were only heading a mile and a half down the road to Clancey's farm. It had been forever since she'd been to the property but Beth talking about it reminded Remington of the track he had on his property. He used to have dirt track races once a month. Even though he wasn't actively having races, he'd kept up the track. When she'd walked it earlier today to check for issues, it had been perfect.

War and she needed to spend time together enjoying each other's company and a little stress relief. She motioned War out of the SUV and walked around to grasp his hand.

"You ready for some fun?"

He twirled her closer, sliding his hand into her hair, claiming her lips. His taste, his touch, had her ignoring everything she planned. A throat clearing had him pulling back.

"War, glad to see you pulled your head out of your ass and saw the perfect woman."

"Mr. Clancey, it's good to see you."

War held his hand out to shake but Mr. Clancey pulled him in tight, slapping his back.

"The side-by-side is stocked and ready to go. Regina dropped off snacks for you and the cooler is in the back. I've got the cattle in the center pasture. They won't care about you all but please make sure the gate is closed securely after you go through. That bull is an instigator and for some reason thinks he needs to enjoy the grass in front of the house."

Remi walked with War but headed to the passenger side. She wanted this enjoyable, and her man did like to be in control. She'd probably pushed every button he had making him let her drive on the way over. War settled behind the wheel and started the vehicle.

"Where to?"

Remington motioned behind the barn. "Follow the track in the grass until we come to the first fence. We'll go through the cattle pasture and then follow the creek to cross at the bridge."

"Dare I ask where we're going or is this one of those things I'm just supposed to roll with?"

She giggled at his aggrieved tone. "Since I know Regina already mentioned Clancey's offer to sell, I thought it would be fun to have some snacks, enjoy an evening together and race on the dirt track."

The smile stretching War's mouth had her admiring his lips and beard. "I'd forgotten about the dirt track and the races. Roam and I used to sneak over with our bikes when we were younger."

"Winnie and I used to do the same until we brought Jesse with us. She brought her skateboard even though we told her it wouldn't work."

War nodded. "I remember. She broke her arm and got us all banned from the track for three months."

"Yep, Mom and Regina were in agreement. Mom grounded Winnie and me for taking our younger sister somewhere dangerous. We got stuck on dish duty for two weeks and Mom gave Jesse this freaking bell that she could ring. We had to get her whatever she wanted when she rang the bell."

Remington closed the last gate and hopped back on, pointing toward the stream. "I'd forgotten how pretty his land was."

A light breeze lifted her hair, making the heat not quite so oppressive.

War followed the stream until he crossed the small bridge, then crested the hill. The racetrack was set down in the pasture. Remington pointed to the bikes waiting at the edge of the track.

"I hope you're ready for a race. I'm not going easy on you, but I will let you choose which bike you want."

War chuckled, his eyes dancing with glee. She'd known this was the perfect way to get him out of the funk he'd been in. He was the MC president, but he needed to realize he couldn't protect everyone. "Rules?"

She'd debated what type of rules to have but in the end, she'd known with War she was safe. Although she really wanted to win just for the bragging rights. When the sale went through, she could imagine the racetrack being used constantly.

"First one across the finish line after five laps wins. Best two out of three races. Work for you?"

He nodded, smirking as he slid on his helmet. She'd told him to wear close-toed shoes along with jeans and some type of long-sleeved jacket. She didn't think they'd wreck but she wasn't taking any chances.

She hid a smile at War doublechecking the bike he'd picked. They pushed them to the starting line, getting on and starting their engines. She held her fingers up, counting down from three to one and then they were off.

War didn't cut her any slack considering they were on a date. He sped up, crossing behind her and took the curve high. She went a little lower and tighter, keeping to the curve. She should feel a little bad that she'd practiced earlier today when she brought the bikes over, but she didn't. All's far in love with War. She'd take any advantage she had because her man was a competitive beast but then, so was she. She couldn't imagine how competitive their kids would be.

When she imagined the future, War was the man in every daydream. Recently, her dreams had included a little boy with War's dark hair and a little girl with his eyes. At her age, kids weren't a guarantee. Whether she was able to carry them, or they adopted, War would make a fantastic father.

She pushed the bike around the last curve. They were neck and neck, but War pushed his a little harder and crossed the finish line right before her. He flipped up his visor, grinning at her.

"This is perfect. Again or do you want a break first?"

Her idea had done exactly what she wanted. War's whole demeanor had relaxed.

"Let's finish the races then we can enjoy the snacks I brought."

He nodded and they backed up behind the starting line.

War leaned against the tree, ruffling his fingers through Remi's hair as she was lying against his leg. He breathed in the fresh air, feeling his shoulders relax. Remi had known what he needed. They'd each won a race then tied on the last one. They'd called it a draw and settled down to eat. Remi's fruit, cheese and summer sausage were perfect. She'd brought tea and water. He'd been a little sweaty after they'd raced so he was thankful she hadn't brought soda.

He could picture the future with Remington, and he knew she wanted one with him, but he wondered what she pictured. Maybe it was time to be a little bolder.

"Do you think about having kids?" he asked, sliding down to settle her more on his shoulder. She'd tensed at the question, then relaxed.

"Did you get mind reading abilities when you were away? I wasn't aware the police department had that capability."

He chuckled, dropping a kiss on her forehead which was still scrunched at him. "Nope, but changing Georgia's diaper and playing outside with Grant and Georgia last night had me thinking about kids today."

She nodded, snuggling into his side. "They are cute and yes, I have."

"With me?"

His whispered question had him irritated with himself. This was his Remi. Who else would she be imagining them with? But with her, the answer meant the world to him. He'd never imagined children with anyone. With Remi, he could see a life here in Bluff Creek. She turned so she could see his face and placed her hands on his cheeks.

"I can't imagine them with anyone else. You're all I can think of, War. I'm not the girly girl but with you, I can see happily ever after and all my dreams coming true."

He gazed at the eyes he could imagine staring into forever as he leaned closer to her mouth. "I plan on making all your dreams come true for the rest of our lives."

Claiming her lips, he rolled on top of her. Her hands slid under his shirt, her nails lightly scraping his back. He shivered. He heartily hoped Clancey stayed away because he was unwrapping the present he'd been gifted. He'd never imagined coming home to Bluff Creek in his forties would give him everything he'd ever wanted. A woman, brothers he loved and maybe someday kids for him to spoil.

Chapter Twenty-Four

After a couple of incidents near the bail bonds company, Remi and War had made the decision to have everyone move to the MC. Although the bail bonds company had more bedrooms, there were too many company people working on the property. Their best bet for containment was all being together. A week with them all living on top of each other had everyone's tempers frayed.

She wasn't sure who, but a couple of the guys had played pranks and her sisters were not happy, hence the text she'd just received.

Winnie: I want to go home. All the man candy is nice to look at, but I'm ready for a break.

Sarah: I'm sorry. Maybe we could sprinkle water on their shoes.

Jesse: Umm, what? I don't think they'd even know you did that. Sarah, you suck at pranks.

Sarah: What if we didn't put their wet clothes in the dryer and just left them?

Remington: Have you been doing their laundry for them? Cause No!

Sarah: I refuse to answer that question.

Winnie: What if we hit them in the nuts until they cry?

Beth: Whoa, where's our sunshine? I think you're too close to this. Although Flick's going to lose something if he doesn't quit using my nice shampoo. It's like thirty bucks a bottle and I have to have it shipped.

She agreed the guys needed to be paid back but it also needed to be enough that they didn't think of retaliation. Right now, she was tired of not having any privacy and of not making any headway. Having to turn away survivors needing help was killing her. What if them turning someone away was the reason someone died? She needed this threat neutralized so they could get back to helping people.

Remington: Okay, let's start off small. Sarah, can you put child locks on their internet so they can't access any adult sites? I'm curious how long it will be until someone mentions it. Don't do it during the day. Wait until midnight to enact it. Jesse, any special contraptions you could make to pay them back?

Jesse: Let me think about it. I'm working on a project for one of the SUVs and will have plenty of time to think.

Remington: Now, everybody get back to work so I can finish the schedule for next month.

Remington kicked back in her chair, contemplating how to keep an all-out war from erupting in the clubhouse. Or maybe she should let it? Maybe everyone could get it out of their systems and be happier.

A snick of the door had her turning toward it and palming her gun. Intellectually, she knew they were safe in the clubhouse but a small part of her never let down her guard. War grinned as he locked the door. Striding toward her, she admired how his tattoos drew attention to his forearms. She loved running her hands up his arms, feeling his muscles underneath and the rasp of his hair against her fingers.

He slid his hands under her arms, lifting her up and tossing her on the bed. She wasn't tiny by any means, but her man made her feel that way.

"To what do I owe the honor?"

"I was sitting there listening to Baron and Locks drone on about something that didn't need my time. I started thinking about your tattoos which led to thinking about my hands on your body and here we are." War's knee hit the bed as he reached up, unbuttoning and unzipping her jeans. "Raise up," he directed. She raised her hips, letting him tug her jeans down and off.

"What are your plans, Mr. President?"

"Hmm, my plans include touching and tasting every spot on your body and making sure we're both satisfied multiple times. Hopefully a couple orgasms will have us both in better moods after dealing with whiny people and the lockdown."

He slipped a finger inside her panties, sliding them down her legs.

"I'd love to forget about whiny people. Do you think they'll miss us if we hide for around forty-eight hours?" She giggled at the look on his face.

"Umm, as long as we rest, I'm sure I could keep you satisfied but I'm not fucking eighteen anymore." He had her top unbuttoned and slid off, with his lips kissing each spot unveiled. "Now, how about less talking and more fucking?"

She could get behind that. Now if everyone could just leave them alone for a minute.

"I think I want to start with this tattoo," War whispered against her skin as he rolled her over and kissed the top of her shoulder blade where her heart and guns tattoo started. "Close your eyes, Remi, and just feel." His tongue started tracing the tattoo. Close her eyes and just feel. She could do that. Her man knew exactly what she needed today.

Chapter Twenty-Five

Remington was itching to ride her bike, but they hadn't lifted security, so she'd be confined to one of the SUVs. Not knowing who was out to get them was frustrating. There was something right at the edge that if she could grab ahold of it, she'd be able to piece everything together.

She grabbed her gun, keys to the SUV and her sunglasses. Tagging herself out and with her location at the tattoo shop increased her bad mood. It annoyed her to have to let someone know where she was every minute of every day.

She'd had her tattoo done earlier this week of Kathryn's Wings, but she'd forgotten she was low on lotion. Getting out and picking up some lotion would give her a break from everyone. Roam had some she particularly liked, and she wanted to talk with him about her next one. She was considering something special regarding War. She'd planned on talking to him about it while she was there before, but his receptionist had left for an emergency right before her appointment. He'd had to answer the phone multiple times because he'd been the only one there.

The drive to the shop didn't relax her but chatting with Roam and just getting out would help. She pushed open the door of the tattoo parlor and analyzed the reception area without thinking twice. The last couple of weeks had changed how vigilant she was. The receptionist wasn't at her desk. Hopefully, Roam wasn't by himself again. He had enough stress in his life with being a single father.

The quiet unnerved her. At this time, the tattoo shop should be bustling with activity. The music that Roam always had playing wasn't on either. She pulled her gun, then texted Code Phoebe at the tattoo shop. They'd all taken to carrying wherever they went. They weren't being caught unaware again.

She walked down the hallway, checking the tattoo stations as she passed. Roam's chair was set up, so he'd obviously been in this morning, but he wasn't there now. Rascal's station was clean. He wasn't working quite as much since he'd turned the majority over to Roam. A scrape from the office had her making her way to the open door, taking her gun in one hand and her phone in the other. A woman who Remi assumed was the receptionist was in front of the wall safe. She flipped on her video, making sure she got the open safe door. The only people allowed in the safe were Roam and Rascal. They didn't trust anyone else. The woman was riffling through what was in there.

Remi would wait and see what she did next. Remi made sure she caught the receptionist's face as she slid the credit union zippered bag out and put it under her arm then pulled a bag of pills out of her front pocket and placed it in the safe. Remi had seen enough because the glimpse of her face had anger coursing through her. What the hell was survivor number five doing in Bluff Creek at the tattoo shop? She couldn't tell if she was armed but Remi wasn't taking any chances. Before the woman could close the safe, Remi stopped the video then walked up behind her, placing her barrel against her back.

"Slowly slide your hands behind you. I don't know why you're messing in the safe, but I know you aren't authorized.

My gun is at your back, and I will shoot if you don't follow my directions. Do you have any weapons on you?"

She squeaked and slid her hands back. Remi made quick work of sliding zip ties on her and pulling her toward the chair beside the desk. Thank goodness her tactical pants aways had items to secure skips. Pushing her down to sit, Remi used another set of zip ties to cuff her hands to the back of the chair.

"Where's Roam?"

Her little thief pursed her mouth, refusing to speak. She'd never liked the little bitch when she came through as a survivor, but she'd chalked it up to the woman's attitude because she was scared.

After she'd secured her, she glanced at her texts. Backup was close but she was worried about where Roam was. Just as she was dialing, the back door banged.

"What the hell, Lora? No one called about the twins being hurt."

The fury and surprise on Roam's face wasn't surprising if she'd used his kids to get rid of him.

"I found her with the safe open removing your money bag and placing a bag of drugs. I was coming to look for you before I questioned her."

Her phone beeped with a text.

Code Chandler

She replied: **Code Joey**

Beth walked in with Winnie, both armed and ready for anything.

"What the hell is she doing in Roam's office?" Winnie asked while Beth scoped out the rest of the shop before coming back. She waited to see how Roam wanted to handle this. She'd prefer calling the sheriff and having him press charges, then waiting to see who came to bail her out.

"What do you mean? Do you know her?"

Winnie nodded at Roam. "She's survivor number five who came through the network. She's supposed to be in Nebraska or letting us know she needed to move. Things seem to be getting interesting."

Remi glared at the woman. "I'm guessing you didn't have an emergency earlier this week. You didn't want me to recognize you. What are you doing here?"

"Not talking to you, bitch."

"Regardless of who she is, I want this handled by the sheriff with a report. Depending on where she needs to go, we might need you to transport," Roam directed. Remington nodded at Beth knowing she'd notify the sheriff. Hopefully he was close because she didn't relish staying any closer to this skank than she had to.

"You better let me go. You're playing with the wrong people."

"Thought you weren't talking," Beth said.

It was funny she thought she had any bargaining power. Although she'd like to tape her mouth closed, she needed her talking. Time to piss her off and see if she'd spout any more information.

"Oh wow! The only thing I'm scared about is getting something contagious from your diseased body," Remi grinned as her words had their thief glaring at her.

"You'll pay. You'll all pay, and you'll wish you'd never stuck your nose into our business."

"What business is that? Skanks are us. Pussy for losers."

Roam's snort had her almost laughing but her words were picking at the woman's self-control. She needed her angry because angry people made mistakes.

"I have one. Travel the love channel. Our channels are the loosest and the last you'll ever have," Beth snickered, barely getting the words out before laughing until tears leaked out of her eyes. Her sisters were the best.

"My turn! My turn!" Winnie yelled. "Ride me for a night of never-ending horrors. Go where everyone has gone before and never gone back for seconds."

Remi kept an eye on their prisoner as her skin turned a mottled shade of red. The sheriff had walked in behind her and nodded at Remi to keep going. She appreciated the way he worked with the bail bonds company and the MC. They were all invested in making Bluff Creek a better place.

"I'm not a fucking skank. I'm in charge of acquisitions, you bitches, and you'll never see the light of day again."

Not what she'd been expecting but enlightening, nonetheless. They knew she was connected to the representative, but the acquisitions comment had her curious.

"I'd like to hear more about your acquisitions. My deputy will take you out to the car while I get some information."

She would have liked to question her a little longer but whatever the sheriff wanted they'd do because he was in charge of the scene now. She was thankful she'd come in when she had. What exactly had the woman planned? Was she planting the drugs to then call a tip in later? What had been her plan? Roam would have known she lied and been furious about the lie about his kids. He would have found the missing money and the drugs when they closed up the register tonight. What was going on and how were they going to stop it?

Chapter Twenty-Six

War kicked the chair when what he wanted to do was hit whoever was screwing with them. He sent a text telling his brothers that council was at four pm. They had a weekly meeting, but this would be their third after the burning of the gym. He knew most MCs called their weekly meetings church, but his mom had put a stop to that when she and Baron first got together. She actually volunteered at the local church and told Baron in no uncertain terms to pick another name. Because Baron adored everything about his woman, he'd of course taken it to his brothers and had changed it within a day.

He was relieved Remington and Roam were both fine, but he was frustrated with constantly playing defense. He and Remington had turned a corner and for the first time in his life, he craved spending time with a woman, his warrior woman. Small times together in the last couple weeks weren't enough. He needed to neutralize the threat, but he'd have to figure out where it was coming from first.

Their little friend who they'd caught was currently hanging out in a special room Baron and his officers had built years ago. They hadn't done anything with him yet besides keep him confined and feed him on a regular basis. War wanted him worried. He also wanted a couple more answers to his questions before he interviewed their friend. Since he didn't have to follow the guidelines of the department, he could have a little latitude with how he did things.

He and the guys had brushed off Remington when she'd asked about him, but he wondered how long she'd be willing to be kept in the dark. He wanted them to be partners, but he wasn't sure if partners meant full disclosure or would she need a little plausible deniability. He didn't plan on killing the guy—just keeping him on ice until he could be used in the most advantageous way.

He'd pushed his bike to the limit getting to the tattoo shop when he'd gotten Remington's text. They'd need to work on their communication. *A little issue at the tattoo shop, giving my statement to the sheriff* wasn't enough. Was anyone hurt? Were shots fired? He'd even worked on memorizing their darn codes but no, his Remi hadn't sent one of those, just some vague shit about an issue. When he'd walked in and seen her whole, his heart had finally started to slow down. He'd walked in, grasped her arms, and pulled her in tight, just holding on for a minute. He hadn't cared he'd interrupted her statement. He'd had to hold her and feel she was okay.

Remington had shoved him out the door when he'd wanted to stay while she went through her statement for the fifth time. She'd promised to come by the clubhouse immediately after. He'd left a prospect with her even though she told him she could take care of herself. He felt better having someone else with her. Her sisters had left to go do what they did best—surveillance and digging into the woman's life. The sheriff had taken the woman to their small Bluff Creek County Jail. Beth had texted that she already had surveillance set up. He'd been surprised to find out Noah had bought the building across from the jail years ago. Upstairs was a small apartment made specifically for surveillance on the jail. The lower level had previously been a law office but had been closed for years.

Even though he'd been scared when he'd received the text, he was thankful Remington had arrived when she had. He hated to think what could have happened to Roam. The drugs had been enough fentanyl to qualify for trafficking. As the owner, Roam would have been liable. Someone wanted them busy playing defense. Even though he knew to follow the leads, his inclination was that this was related to the other events. He should have been working the issue, going back over all the information, but he was wired. He couldn't decide whether he wanted to go to the range to take out his rage or to go pound on a bag for a while. He'd obviously had rose-colored glasses when he imagined coming home to the MC. He'd envisioned leading his men and bringing scumbags to justice. Dealing with threats and feeling helpless hadn't ever entered his mind.

He checked his phone again to see if Remi had texted she was done. He needed to hold her in his arms. She'd promised to talk with him. A click at the door had him pausing. Crap. Even in his own clubhouse, he was uneasy.

Remington walked in, glanced around the room, then turned and locked the door.

"I thought you were going to text when you were done." His tone had her pausing, cocking an eyebrow. Okay, maybe he could have sounded a little less petulant. "Sorry." Watching his parents, he knew you didn't let that crap fester. He wasn't too proud to apologize when he was an ass.

"I would have but I was so ready to leave, and I wasn't alone. Roam rode his bike back behind my SUV. Is my man a little cranky?"

He loved her calling him her man but cranky sounded like he was a fucking toddler. He was frustrated, irritated and furious that Remington hadn't been safe going to the tattoo shop. He slid the chair back, starting to stand, needing to feel her. Her palm on his chest pushed him back down.

"Wha..."

Her lips cut off his question, taking his mouth, letting him experience her taste. Her hand sliding down his chest had him grabbing her back, trying to lift her onto him.

"Uh-uh," she shook her finger at him. "I have something else in mind, Mr. President, to help you refocus."

He nodded, waiting to see what she had planned next. He hoped it included him inside her because his dick was almost painful behind his jeans. Seconds in Remi's presence and he was ready.

Her hands had his belt undone and his zipper opened. Her hand grasping him had him thrusting up toward her, sliding his jeans down along with his briefs. Her thumb ran along the underside, touching each of his Jacob ladder piercings. His eyes widened as she dropped to her knees.

"I've been wanting to taste you and I'm curious about how you'll feel in my mouth. I assume you're okay with me satisfying my curiosity?"

He nodded because he wasn't sure he had enough moisture in his mouth to talk. Seeing Remington's dark hair spill onto his thighs as she leaned close to him had him tensing. The first touch of her tongue on the underside of his shaft had him counting backwards, trying not to blow before she had him in her mouth.

She licked, her tongue investigating each piercing while her thumb rubbed the moisture leaking around his head. Remi's tongue bathed the top of his head before she enveloped him, letting him bump the back of her throat. He grasped her hair, trying to hold back but then realized he was fighting a losing battle. The woman he loved had his hips thrusting into her mouth.

"Remi?"

She pulled back just enough to lick around the crown. "War, this is for you. Do whatever feels good."

She engulfed him in her warm, wet mouth, lashing his piercings with her tongue, her hand sliding and squeezing until he couldn't remember why he was irritated. He thrust into her mouth a couple times then let go. Remi swallowed around him as he came, her eyes on his. Could he love this woman any more than he did? It wasn't because she'd given him the best blowjob of his life. She knew him. Knew the frustration he'd had over the situation and had decided she'd give of herself to take it away. She was the other half of his heart. The piece he hadn't known he'd needed. He lifted her onto his lap after she tucked him in.

"I didn't take care of you."

Her smile lit his world. Her hand rubbed along his beard before she kissed his lips. "Sometimes taking care of you is enough. Knowing I can give that to you gives me pleasure. Do you feel a little less out of control?"

He shook his head and grinned at her. "Yes. My woman knows exactly how to take care of her man."

He sat for a moment, relaxing, holding Remington. Her head on his shoulder and her hand patting his cut.

"We'll get through this, War. I have complete faith that we'll find that one piece of information that will give us what we need. Her being at Roam's shop might help Sarah and Scoop find that small thread that leads to another one. The answer may not be when we'd like it but as long as we have each other, we'll get through anything."

He knew they could get through anything together. He wanted to make sure it was before anyone else was hurt. The thought of anyone in his family being hurt scared him, no, fucking petrified him. He couldn't let anyone else down.

"I think we need to all meet. There's too many pieces crossing over."

War nodded. "I agree. How about I move council back two hours and we'll have it be everyone involved. It will give Scoop and Sarah a little time to research. Since this includes Kathryn's Wings, how do you want to handle it?"

She nodded, leaning on his shoulder. "Even though it worries me, I think we have to trust the rest of the MC brothers with the project. If we don't, their input won't be valid because they'll only have half the pieces. I always planned on everyone but your prospects knowing, so now's as good as time as any. And way to go, baby, for asking me instead of demanding I do something."

Her giggle at the end of her speech had him shaking his head. He could admit he'd been a complete ass early on. "I may be older, but I can learn. My warrior woman is an asset and can do anything she sets her mind to."

Despite how frustrated he was with everything, he'd never been more content. Remington in his arms and knowing they had a future. Now, he had to fucking figure out how to make sure the threat to their future was gone.

Chapter Twenty-Seven

Remington scrutinized everyone coming in, ensuring they were part of the MC. She and War had decided on only her dad and her sisters from the bail bonds or security company. She hated to doubt any of their employees, but they didn't have the same level of family at the bail bonds and security company that the brotherhood did.

Once everyone had found a seat, War nodded. Bear locked the doors while Scoop turned on a couple of devices.

"I know this is unusual for a meeting with the women but bringing us all together is the only way we'll figure this out. Scoop and Sarah are going to start us off with current pictures of people we've had problems with. We aren't assuming anything is related but we need to see everything."

He nodded and Scoop started, motioning at the TV on the wall. "Okay, this is the security company's client who set up Bear and Remington. He's listed under this name," Scoop motioned to the first name in a list, "but after Sarah and I dug further, none of the names are what he was on his birth certificate. His paperwork is good. I can see how he made it this far but his birth name is Kevin McBaine."

"While Rocky Road dug into the client, I dug into survivor number five. On the surface everything looks good, which is why she passed our initial check. We didn't do deep dives because we assumed everyone coming to us was in a bad situation. After a little research, she and Kevin have a lot in common. Multiple names that all lead back to a birth name which disappeared from existence over forty years ago. Meet Lucinda McBaine, Kevin's younger sister."

A chorus of what the fucks and grumbling had Sarah pausing.

Scoop shushed the group. "Can you guys shut it and let her finish?" Scoop growled.

"Digging deeper, we uncovered the same mother for them—Suzanne McBaine. No father is listed on the birth certificate. We were able to find a current picture of Suzanne and a couple from the seventies and eighties. Here's her picture."

In the older pictures, the woman had long brown hair and was dressed in tight tank tops along with an MC cut. The picture was grainy and the MC logo on the cut was blurred.

"Do we know what MC she's connected with?" Remington asked, pausing when she noticed her dad and Baron staring at each other. She hated when they seemed to talk to each other without words. It came from them serving together but it was still irritating.

"So do you all want to share with the rest of us?"

Baron motioned to Locks to go ahead. When they were still trying to decide who would update them, Rascal jumped in.

"Suzanne was a club girl in the early days of the club. She went by Paradise."

"What a misnomer that was. She named herself," Locks offered.

"Why don't I remember her?" Regina questioned.

Baron shook his head and rolled his eyes. "She was before you came here. She was messing around with..." Baron paused.

"She was messing around with who?" War stood and banged his hand on a table. "This fucking concerns all of us. If you're hiding something, it needs to stop."

Locks motioned for War to sit, and he stood up. "It's something we're not proud of but it's time it's out there. When we originally formed Bluff Creek Brotherhood MC, there were seven of us from the Army that came here. The majority of us were in agreement which way we wanted the MC to go. We thought everyone was but behind our backs, one of the members began making moves. He'd been named Sneak in the military for the way he could get into enemy camps. Unfortunately, his name was truer than we knew. He didn't want the life we all did. He wanted to run drugs and women—whether they were willing or not. Paradise saw dollar signs and did everything to become his old lady. I was distracted with starting the bail bonds company and Kathryn and I had just been married."

Noah paused and Baron motioned for him to sit. "Locks was the one of us with a woman, so he was vulnerable. Kathryn didn't like Suzanne, but she wasn't the type of woman to be mean just for the sake of it. When Suzanne dropped by the house needing to talk to Kathryn, she didn't suspect a thing. When Kathryn's back was turned, Suzanne knocked her out. They took your mom and hid her. Sneak walked into church and told us how we were going to run the MC, or he was giving Kathryn to someone as a gift. Sneak may have been smart in some ways, but he considered women commodities. He left Paradise as the only guard. While Sneak was giving us his ultimatum, Kathryn had convinced Paradise to untie her for the bathroom. She knocked out Paradise, took her gun and car. She wasn't sure who all Sneak had on his side, but she knew Clancey and his wife. She stopped there. Clancey called Dan and the three of them burst into church. Kathryn didn't give Sneak a chance to explain anything. She shot as soon as the door was open. She was an amazing shot and took part of his hand off. We called the sheriff and let the law handle it. We warned him to never come back, or he wouldn't leave breathing. He died in prison a couple years later."

"So their kids are coming back at us? If he went to jail, how did he father Suzanne's kids? I still think we're missing a lot," Remington stated.

"I'm not sure how this all goes together. Let's let Sarah and Scoop do some more research into Sneak and Paradise. We're all tired, irritated, and not thinking straight with everything going on. Scoop, Sarah, how long do you need before we could meet again?"

"War, this is a lot of info. I'm not sure." Sarah nodded at Scoop's words.

"Okay, everybody stay vigilant. We'll meet when they have more for us."

Remington waited as the members chatted with War. She'd known her mom was strong but hadn't realized how badass she really was. She'd known she was an incredible shot because her mom and dad had both taught her and her sisters how to shoot.

She had too many questions still. What was the end goal? Why try to take out the MC and the security company? Did they have a competing company? Why did it make a difference if the MC and the security company existed and what changed if they didn't?

Her head was starting to hurt from all the questions and stress. War sauntered over to her, brushing her hair off her forehead when he stopped in front of her.

"Headache?"

"Yes," she answered, keeping her head still. It had progressed to her neck and movement was bothering her. War's arm went around her as he placed a light kiss against her forehead.

"So sleep for you. Where would be best?"

"Let's do your room. I can sleep and get rid of this headache, and you can spend time with your brothers. They'll need to talk after all the revelations."

"And that's why you're perfect for me. Let's get you a hot pack for your head, meds and a dark room."

Remi let him lead her to his room. She'd worry tomorrow about how to stop the threat. With her man and her family, they'd conquer this threat. She only hoped no one else was hurt before they did.

Chapter Twenty-Eight

It had been a week since they'd found out about Sneak. Sarah and Scoop had been working around the clock without any breaks. War and she had discussed everyone needed a break. She'd suggested a party, but War had pushed for them to go to Dodge City.

They'd left a small group protecting both compounds. They were using SUVs and motorcycles. She was riding with War while her sisters brought another SUV. War had kept secret where they were going but when they pulled into the bar they were banned from, she doubled up her fist and hit his shoulder.

"I'm not freaking walking in there and getting kicked out."

He chuckled and shook his head. "Seriously, you honestly think I'd set you up for that?"

No, she didn't but Whiskey, Hennessey and Schaefer had been ballistic over Jesse's antics, and it would take a lot for them to forgive and forget. She really missed the bar, though, because they had themed nights with trivia, karaoke, and the food was great.

War tapped her thigh, waiting for her to get off the bike. She got off and unbuckled her helmet, shaking her hair out after she took it off. The cacophony of her sisters screeching about where they were hurt her ears.

"What the hell, War? Are you thinking it would be fun to watch us get kicked out? Are you trying to have Jesse be embarrassed tonight?" Winchester growled while glaring.

"Hey, War's got it covered. As far gone as he is for Remington, do you honestly think he'd allow his woman and her sisters to be embarrassed?" Bear shook his head, rolling his eyes then stomping toward the door. Yanking it open, he held it, motioning for them all to go in. "Oh, for Pete's sake, what the fuck are you waiting for?"

Remington hid a smile at Winnie storming through the door, shoving his chest as she went through. She waited for War to get off the motorcycle and curl his arm around her.

"I've got this. We're going to have a fun time drinking, dancing, and laughing. Nobody is hurting my warrior woman."

She trusted War. It was the Nelson brothers she wasn't sure about. She could understand their egos being hurt but Jesse didn't date them at the same time. She'd gone on a couple dates with each of them with about three weeks between each brother. She hadn't been serious about any of them, at least as far as Remi knew, but that hadn't stopped them from comparing notes and banning the girls from the saloon.

She stepped into the bar, spotting Whiskey behind the bar eyeing them as they all walked in.

"Your tables are reserved by the dance floor, but your payment isn't here yet."

"Thanks, Whiskey. It should be here momentarily. They texted there was a wreck blocking both lanes for about an hour."

Whiskey nodded and turned around to cash out a customer. It was a little anticlimactic but whatever War had done to fix this, she was ecstatic. War kept his hand against her back as they crossed the floor. She hadn't ever allowed a man that liberty but with War, it wasn't trying to control her. He was showing her he valued her and wanted to stay in contact with her, even in a crowded bar. Not that her man wasn't above staking a claim if he felt like men weren't respecting his woman. His protective nature coupled with his badass attitude was something she loved about him now.

War pulled out her chair and waited until she was settled before taking his seat. A waitress walked over, ready to take their order.

"We'll all have water until the delivery gets here but we'd like to go ahead and get the appetizers I ordered while everyone checks out the menu." She nodded and left.

She was going to ask what order he was talking about, but he stood and grinned toward the door.

"Special delivery, and you all better fucking appreciate it because traffic was a bitch and it's fucking hot. Who was the asshole that decided we needed to keep it cold all the way here?"

War chuckled. "The asshole would be me. Whiskey, we'll all take a cold one."

Whiskey nodded and started helping Gage unload the delivery. Remi arched her brow, wondering what was going on.

"When your man was groveling and decided he needed to make up for being a jackass, he sent me to the brothers to find out what it would take for them to allow all of you back in the bar." Bear paused dramatically and frowned when no one clamored for more. "You all suck sometimes. They requested that they get to sell Bluff Creek Brews at their bar for at least a year and the first order was free."

Remi slid her hand up to War's face. This man continued to surprise her. He was the tough president when he needed to be, but he had a soft center where she was concerned. She leaned over, tasting his lips.

Just like every time they touched, his lips had her forgetting she was planning a quick kiss and she wanted to slide her hands under his shirt. The catcalls and laughter had War's lips pulling back from her.

"To be continued..."

She nodded. Oh yes, they would be continuing as soon as she could get home. She just hoped they made it home and didn't get caught somewhere along the side of the road. Her man was potent, and she wasn't sure how long she could wait.

Whiskey and the waitress brought over the beers, handing them out to everyone with Whiskey taking one for himself.

"I'd like to propose a toast. May our memories of regrets be short. May our joy in the moment be sweet and may our partnership be a smooth road. To Bluff Creek Brews and Nelson's Honkytonk Saloon and Bar."

Remi took a drink of her beer. Beer wasn't her favorite but this one had her changing her mind. She wasn't sure what flavor was making her want more but this might be her new favorite drink. The appetizers were delivered, and they dug in.

War watched his woman laughing and chatting with everyone. For a little while, he could enjoy time and not think about their problems. He wasn't naïve, though. He had a couple of brothers stationed outside the bar watching for any threats.

He was glad he was able to give this to his woman. Although there were other bars in Dodge City, he trusted

Whiskey and his brothers to help keep them safe. He'd had Scoop do research on the three brothers, their dad, his brother, and the cousins who owned the bar before having Bear approach about what it would take to allow the sisters back.

Besides the beer, he'd offered all the owners a discount on any work at the brotherhood's garage for a year. He'd done the numbers. Even with the discount, if they all took him up on it for their motorcycles alone, it would be profitable.

Remington's hand slid along and patted his arm. He'd never been big on girls who hung all over him but with Remington, he wanted it all. Having her touch him casually was comforting. Of course, if she started rubbing her fingers elsewhere, he'd be adjusting himself. But he would anyway because he planned on dancing with his woman once they finished eating.

He'd take any excuse to hold her close and have her in his arms. She was close to finishing her last bites and the need to have her in his arms was building. He wondered if in twenty years he'd still feel this all-consuming need to have her close. He hoped so. He dreamed of having what his parents had and with Remington, he knew it was possible.

Remington wiped her mouth with her napkin. He turned toward her, leaning close to her ear. "I need to hold you. Will you dance with me?"

At her nod, he stood and had them on the dance floor before anyone at the table could draw them into another conversation.

"Impatient, much?"

Pulling Remington flush against him, he nibbled her ear as he swayed to the music. "Yes," he whispered. Remington leaned close and licked along his jawline. "Two can play this game. I thought we were dancing, not driving each other insane."

"Can't it be both?"

Swaying to the music, having Remi running her hands along his back was perfect. When he came back to Bluff Creek, he'd never imagined he'd be in this place with this woman. They fit, somehow. The next slow song started, and he saw a couple of her sisters talking with the DJ. They'd have a hard time getting the music changed to anything else. He'd paid the DJ ahead of time to have a minimum of six slow songs when he and Remington got on the dance floor.

The DJ must have ratted him out because her sisters were marching over to where they were dancing.

"What the fuck, War?" Jesse screeched. "I finally get in here again and they're all slow songs."

"They're not all slow songs. We have three more left to dance to then he can play anything else. Go grab the guys. They're not going to say no to holding a woman on the dance floor."

Jesse stomped off while Winnie glared at War for a minute. "Did Regina put you up to this? She's trying to get everybody together."

He shook his head, feeling Remington chuckling into his neck. "No but if I thought I'd win brownie points with her, then I would have. I've finally got off of the shit list I was on when I was mean to Remi. I'm not getting back on it. Now, go or I'll pay him another fifty bucks for more slow songs."

He chuckled at her attitude. He could see he'd never be bored with having Remington's sisters involved in their lives.

Remington's hand slid up into his hair, her fingers scratching his scalp.

"Are you laughing at my sisters?"

"Maybe a little. Wondering how much trouble they'll cause with their antics."

Remington rubbed her breasts against his chest. "Maybe not but we could find men for them, so they were busy elsewhere."

How the hell was he supposed to concentrate on her words when he wanted to rip off her top and feel her skin to skin?

"I am ecstatic with you, woman, but I don't want to mess in my brothers' lives."

He tried to sound stern to discourage Remington but honestly, all he cared about was how she was moving against him. She could ask him to do anything at this point and he'd say yes if it meant they could be skin on skin. How this woman could make him fall in love with every part of her amazed him.

Her grin and how she snorted before going into a full-on belly laugh never failed to bring a smile to his face. The way she paid attention to a conversation no matter what was going on. The originals all loved chatting with her because she listened to them and made them feel valued. In fact, if he didn't know better, he'd think Rascal was trying to steal her away as many times as he found them discussing life.

And definitely don't get between her and someone hurting her sisters. When Jesse mentioned the delivery guy had refused to leave the order with her at the garage, he thought Remington was going to go scorched earth on the company. She and her sisters could do all sorts of crap to each other, but they banded together when someone crossed a line.

He wanted to build a life with Remington. He was excited for what was ahead of them, but he didn't want this threat hanging over them. He couldn't make life worry free for Remi, but he was going to try his hardest to make it easier. She meant the world to him and if making her life easier by smoothing the way at her favorite bar did it, he'd make it happen.

The last slow song ended and as the beat started of the next song, her sisters grabbed Remington, pulling her away from him.

"Girls' dance, War."

"Walk away, dude."

"You can have her later."

The comments flew fast and furious. If he wanted these women on his side, he needed to give them their time alone. He found it incredibly humorous, though, that they'd picked "I Wanna Dance With Somebody" as the song to not allow him to dance with his woman.

He started to head toward the bar when Whiskey's brother Hennessey grabbed the man War had clocked holding tight to the waitress. Hennessey lifted him off his feet and threw him out the door one of the cousins held open.

Whiskey walked over and wiped away a five from a white board and wrote zero. When Whiskey moved back, War could see the words above it. *Days since we've booted an asshole from the saloon.*

As he learned more about Whiskey and his family, he wondered if they might be a solution to their membership numbers. All Whiskey's brothers and cousins rode motorcycles. They also had no problem dealing with issues.

"War, get over here and let me beat you at pool," Bear called.

He wanted to get to know the brothers a little more before he brought the question to council. From what he knew, they were good men, but did they have what it took? He wanted good men who didn't mind bending the rules a little to teach a lesson sometimes. Leaving the force was the best thing to happen to him.

He'd go play a little pool, check how his brothers were doing and enjoy watching his woman shake and move on the dance floor. Then he'd take her home, hers or his didn't matter, and give her enough orgasms, she'd forget her own name.

Chapter Twenty-Nine

War kept quiet while Remington entered an update on her computer for their security detail. After another month without any headway, they'd relaxed the rules a little. Kathryn's Wings was still not accepting new survivors, but they'd all got back to work.

He and Remington had finally gotten to work together on a security gig. He'd worried a little he'd screw up the headway he and Remington had made by trying to take control. When they'd met, Remington had everything planned to the tiniest detail. Her plans were exactly what he'd done, and he'd followed her without hesitation.

They both were ready to be at home after six days away and were driving from Wellington back to Bluff Creek. Remington was all business on the trip, and he agreed but he missed the taste and feel of his woman.

They'd just passed Medicine Lodge and were in the hills between it and Coldwater. Although the land was beautiful, he despised not being able to see what was on the road over the next hill. The sun wasn't far enough down to be able to see headlights coming.

He was loving the SUVs Jesse had modified. Besides being bulletproof, it had all sorts of features and cubbies to hold weapons and gear. If he had to be inside a vehicle, it wasn't a bad one to drive. Remington finished up inputting in the computer and shut it, folding the computer tray flat and then down by her seat.

He wasn't speeding but he seemed to be gaining on the semi-truck in front of them.

"Is he even going forward? If he's having trouble, he needs to get off the road."

He nodded, agreeing with Remi, but something didn't feel right. Remington reached behind him, grabbing their vests. She slipped hers on then leaned over, helping him put his on.

"Something's off. I texted the group. There are two vehicles coming up fast behind us."

"You think they're going to try to box us in?"

"Yeah, look at the drop off on this hill. I mean we could drive it but you'd have to hit the angle just right to minimize rolling over."

"Suggestions?" War asked.

They were still about one hundred yards from the semi and it was stopped. The drop off for the ditch on their side was steep but the other side didn't look as bad. It looked like he could pass but he couldn't imagine they hadn't thought of that. Either something big was waiting on the other side of the hill or they had some other plan.

"I think you act like you're going to pass as if we don't know anything is wrong. At the last minute, drive into the ditch on the left. Hopefully, if they have anything on the other side of the hill, they didn't plan for the ditch. If they did, play it by ear."

Remington had her gun out and ready and pulled a rifle from the back seat.

"I'm only shooting if I need to, but I'll have to roll down the window if I do."

War clicked the turn signal on, looking as if he was passing the stalled vehicle. The two vehicles behind were gaining but were still about fifty feet back. War couldn't decide if he should speed up or slow down because they both had risks. He drove up the hill.

"Ditch, ditch now!" Remington yelled.

He jerked the wheel toward the left, sending them across a gravel driveway at the top of the hill and into the ditch. The staccato beat of multiple guns firing along with the sounds of their impact in the car had him looking for more threats.

"Back on the road, now," Remington directed, keeping an eye out for them.

"Their first plan didn't work but we have no idea if they have more. I say floor it and go. The closer we can get to home, the more chance we'll have for backup."

War had his foot to the floor and the SUV was going fast but the hills weren't making it easy.

"How far away is backup?"

"Sarah estimated ten minutes but we're moving closer to them so hopefully less. I so wish there was some place to hide along here but there's nothing."

He glanced toward Remi to see how she was handling it though he knew she was calm in the crisis and glimpsed a vehicle racing toward them off the side driveway.

"Brace!" he yelled.

Remington opened her eyes, but something was dripping on her face. She tried to swipe it away. What had happened?

"Remi, wake up." A hand patted her leg. "Come on, wake up. They'll be here in a second."

With his words, everything was clear. The vehicle hit them. She could see out of one eye. Their SUV had been knocked into the ditch but was still facing upright at least.

"The windows are intact although I'm not sure how or for how long."

The watches went off. "Remi, War, are you okay?"

"Code Ross."

"We have your location and backup is minutes away. We just need you to hold on." Sarah's calming voice helped but it could all be over in minutes.

"Guys, this is Jesse. I installed a new item but didn't have time to test before you took it. Both middle seats will shift up and back. There'll be a gun underneath and a switch. Ideally, the switch will open a small opening where the gun can fire out. It hasn't been tested so it could work, or it might not."

Considering the situation they were in, she'd try anything. War unbuckled and crawled through the seats. He flipped up the seat and shifted it back. Flipping the switch, he moved closer to use the gun.

"Remi, you need to unbuckle and get down. I'm waiting until they're close enough, it's fatal. Once they know we have it, they could just avoid it."

She unbuckled and slid closer to the floor. She flicked the rearview mirror to see the area they were coming from. After working on security with War, they knew each other's moves like they'd worked together forever. Sometimes he took the lead and sometimes she did. With the blood dripping down her face and her vision being off a little, she was thankful War was in charge of the gun. If they got the glass to break, then she'd fire but for now, she'd be the spotter.

"They're coming down the hill. I count three, no, four. One's staying behind on the road. Thirty feet away."

Night had fallen fast. The sun had dipped down, and everything was dark besides their headlights and the headlights of the vehicles on the road. The assailants were shadows moving closer. Why the heck did everything seem sinister at night? She hoped there were only four, but she couldn't see all around the SUV, and she also didn't want to give away her location in the vehicle.

"Twenty feet away."

The three paused at about fifteen feet away, talking among themselves with lots of gestures.

"They're fifteen feet away and waiting. I think now is the best time to hit them."

War took a deep breath, blowing out loud enough for her to hear. "Let's hope this gun works." The silence was unnerving but once War fired, everything would change.

War cranked the mini gatling gun. The sound in the enclosed space had Remi wishing for ear plugs. She couldn't imagine how loud it was for War right on top of it.

The bullets hit a couple targets and two of the people had fallen down, screaming. She bet that hurt but she didn't have any sympathy for them. They were trying to kill her and War. Whatever happened, they were getting what they deserved. If War couldn't keep them away, she'd lower the window and shoot but she agreed with War. Right now, the vehicle was their best bet on survival. Their attackers had picked the perfect spot halfway between Medicine Lodge and Coldwater with help too far away. The third assailant turned to run up the ditch, trying to dodge the fire from War. The man on the road turned, shooting back at them. Remi lost track of how many bullets hit the vehicle.

"Code Chandler," a voice directed.

War's rapid fire from the gatling gun paused. Gunfire from the road filled the air until there was only silence.

"Code Joey," Sarah's voice was a welcome sound.

Targets neutralized. It was almost too good to be true. She'd had thoughts of War and her dying on this stretch of road and there were so many things she wanted to say to him. She sat up, looking over the seat at War.

"Are you okay?"

He nodded. "I think I'm better than you. You've got a cut on your forehead. The airbags did their job. Let me crawl over and see if we can get out this back door."

War got a door open, and she crawled over to follow him out the door. She walked over to the first body, then let War help her up out of the ditch to the second body. Now that she was upright, she was a little nauseous. Lucinda and Suzanne McBaine were dead. Despite the blood, she recognized both of them. There was one more body on the road and then Sarah had a man cuffed and sitting against an SUV. She was holding a gun on him while Scoop was taking a picture of the body on the road.

"You guys okay?" Sarah asked.

Before Remington could answer, Scoop was motioning them over to the body. "You guys need to see this."

War and she looked at the body then at Scoop's computer identifying the man.

"That doesn't make any sense. Dad said he was dead," War said, shaking his head. "How is that possible?"

Scoop's computer identified the body as Lester McBaine, aka Sneak.

"I know that's what they said but his fingerprints come back to Sneak, and I put his old picture in the computer and aged it. Facial recognition is ninety percent positive this is Lester McBaine. Plus, look at his hand. Locks said Kathryn shot off part of it. He's missing part of his left hand. The guy over there isn't talking and his prints have been removed. I'm guessing hired muscle. I don't know who died in prison, but I'm positive it wasn't Lester McBaine."

Remington paused. She was tired, hurt and wasn't thinking clearly. She wasn't even sure what they should do next. Sirens heralded a sheriff's SUV and an ambulance. She wanted to give a statement, go home, take a hot shower then fall into bed.

"How'd you and Sarah get here so quick?" War questioned.

"She'd found an old address for Suzanne in Medicine Lodge, and we were heading to check it out. Everyone else was at least an hour away or more."

Remington patted Scoop's shoulder. "Thanks, not sure we would have made it otherwise."

She walked over to Sarah and waited until the sheriff had put the cuffed man in his cruiser. Then Sarah grabbed her and pulled her in for a hug.

"I'm so glad you're okay."

"Only thanks to you finding an address for Suzanne. If you guys hadn't been close, this would have been a different outcome. He say anything before you handed him off?"

"No. Did Scoop identify the bodies?"

"Yes. The only one noticeably absent is Kevin McBaine." She paused when Sarah brushed her hair back and held something against her forehead. "Could you stop it? That hurts." Remington tried to bat Sarah's hand away.

"Quit acting like a baby. Your cut is bleeding into your eye. I swear, for being such a badass, you are a big baby when you're hurt."

Oh no, she didn't just call her a big baby. Those were fighting words in their family. Sarah needed a reminder who was in charge.

"Listen, Sarah..."

Sarah's hand over her mouth stopped her. "There's the Remington I know and love. You looked a little like you were going into shock. Nothing like getting angry at your sister to get the blood and adrenaline pumping again." Sarah's smirk had her wanting to smack it off her face in the ring. Oh yeah, they didn't have a ring right now.

She just wanted for everything to go back to normal, well, normal with the addition of War in her life. She wouldn't give him up for anything. She missed working out at the gym. Winnie had a home gym, but it wasn't the same. She missed the students she helped, too. Not being able to hang out with them was hard. She'd worry about all the things they needed to work on tomorrow. As long as she was cleared, she was heading home, and War was going to be sleeping right beside her. She needed her man's arms around her to remind her they were alive.

Chapter Thirty

War watched from the van, keeping an eye on the front door of the bar. Whiskey had promised to let them know when it looked like the meeting was breaking up. Scoop and Sarah had worked around the clock and forty-eight hours after the attack, they'd found a small thread that tied Kevin to an MC from Oklahoma who was rumored to run drugs and be involved in human trafficking.

This was one of those times when War was okay skirting the law. These men would never go to jail for the crimes they actually committed so War was helping them out. Cannon had secured enough marijuana, fentanyl, and meth to qualify for multiple trafficking charges. They'd be calling in with a tip that they'd seen drugs exchanged. War only wanted Kevin. He was the lynchpin to keeping Remi and their family safe. If he could get anyone else, he'd consider it a bonus.

War gave the sign and Ambush from their Texas chapter casually moved through the parking lot. If War wasn't looking for him and knew where he was going to be going, he'd never have spotted him. He wanted someone no one could connect with the MC but also had the skills to accomplish the task. Whiskey coincidentally had his cameras unavailable due to an upgrade running. In under three minutes, Ambush was giving the sign they were good to go. Now it was a waiting game. He texted Whiskey the outside part had been accomplished.

While Ambush would be heading back, their Texas chapter's construction company would be coming for an extended stay. The land purchase had gone through, and Beth's plans had been approved. The construction company would be working on modifying the existing barn into a gym. They'd set aside two areas for houses for the MC members. His parents were going to stay in their current house until the houses farther inside the property could be built. Then their house would become additional housing for visitors.

After everything they'd been through, he was ready for those with families to be farther inside the property. The MC had voted to also look at opening the racetrack for additional income. His mom was doing a cost analysis. He'd really misjudged her. She was an amazing businesswoman and he made sure he showed her.

"War, heads up," Bear whispered while smacking his shoulder. He had been daydreaming a little. He needed to keep his head in the game. Kevin walked out first and got in his car to leave. Bear messaged Scoop to make the call. He was routing it through a couple places so it couldn't be traced. Bear waited until their target drove a little ahead. War was positive Kevin was too cocky to think he had a tail, but you never knew how paranoid someone was. As Kevin drove through the light, a police K-9 SUV flashed their lights, pulling him over. Bear pulled their car over and parked by another car. The officer got out, walking up to Kevin's car. Another police cruiser pulled in front of the vehicle, blocking it in. The officer got out, walking up to the right of the vehicle. As he approached, Kevin must have realized how big a deal this was and decided he wanted no part of it.

War watched in amazement as Kevin's car backed up, hitting the police SUV, then tried to turn. He was pinned in but must have decided anything was worth it and drove his car up onto the sidewalk. One officer was screaming at him to stop while the other ran to his car, trying to head off Kevin's car on the sidewalk. A third police car with sirens wailing sped by, pulling up onto the sidewalk so Kevin couldn't reverse.

"We should have popcorn. This guy is an idiot," Bear grumbled.

War agreed. Kevin didn't know they'd planted drugs so why was he hell-bent on not stopping for the police? He must have decided he couldn't go anywhere because he'd stopped the car and had his hands out the driver's side window. The officers cuffed him and read him his rights. Two of the officers started searching and found the stash they'd placed in the center console and under the driver's seat. The officer opening the trunk reared back when he opened it. The officer who had been standing by the cuffed Kevin had to tackle him when Kevin tried to run away.

Then two officers were helping a tied-up woman out of the trunk. War had never been so glad he'd bent the rules and had Ambush place the drugs. If they hadn't called in the tip, who knew where the woman would have ended up and what would have been done to her. Sometimes, the right thing to do didn't always mean it was law-abiding. War watched a little longer then motioned to Bear to leave.

He had a burning need to hold Remington in his arms and show her how much she meant to him. He'd been burnt out and disillusioned when he left the force. He'd known the MC having a purpose would help with that but more than that, it was Remi. She was the light in his life when he could see only darkness. They may have started off a little rocky, but he wouldn't change a thing.

He appreciated everything about her because he knew how easy it was to lose what you loved. He'd been petrified when they'd been attacked on the road. In seconds, he could have lost his everything, but they'd been lucky backup was close by. He wanted it all with Remington; kids, a house, and a long life, plus tall fences with barbed wire to keep his family safe. Remi would be all over the tall fences, but she mentioned she wasn't living anywhere that resembled a prison. He guessed he could understand that.

Wow. Kids with Remi. She took his breath away when she was in her motorcycle boots, tight jeans, leather jacket and sunglasses but imagining her pregnant had him trying to surreptitiously adjust himself.

"Quit thinking about your woman."

Bear sounded grouchier than normal. He'd tried to check in on how Bear was doing now that they'd been home for a while. Bear had made it clear he had a dad and didn't need War acting like one.

"It's hard. She's absolutely perfect."

Bear chuckled as he backed out of the parking space. "Yeah, it is, and I don't need to see it but at least you finally got your head out of your ass and saw what you had in front of you."

Sometimes having a best friend who knew you too well was fucking annoying.

"Take us home, asshole, I'm ready to see my woman."

Chapter Thirty-One

Remington glanced at the newly painted walls and new flooring. It had taken a couple of months, but the gym was finished and officially opening. She was alone in the building because in Winnie's excitement, she'd forgotten her clothes to wear after they were done with set-up. She'd taken one of the side-by-sides back to her house.

With the addition of the acreage they'd bought and the fencing that had been installed, they'd purchased eight side-by-sides for each large building on the property. If Winnie avoided the pasture where the cattle were then she'd only need to open one gate.

Remington had worried she'd feel uncomfortable being by herself in the gym but with the safeguards they'd put in place and Kevin in jail, she wasn't. She wasn't sure what all had gone on but with the charges against him, he'd taken a plea deal. The woman in his trunk hadn't said anything when rescued by police and had disappeared from the hospital when left alone in the room. Kevin would spend a long time in jail if he survived his stay. In the plea deal, Kevin had been required to admit everything he'd done. He'd admitted he and his mom had gotten a body from a morgue and paid the warden of the prison to release Sneak and report the body as his. The warden had died five years ago so he wouldn't pay for his part.

Now, if she could get her man to move them to the next level then everything would be friggin' perfect. They took turns spending the night together when they were able, but she'd like them to be official. Deciding whose place to spend the night in was getting tiresome, especially when War picked his. He'd moved into a small cottage that came available next door to his parents. She didn't mind being close, but the cottage was small—one bedroom, one bathroom and a kitchen/living room. Granted, it was better than his room in the clubhouse but not by much. She'd had enough of that during their lockdown after they'd been attacked. She was still dealing with the fallout of that. At the sound of a text, she rolled her eyes. And there they were again.

Jesse: Payback is happening. Remi - you should make sure you and War stay at your house tonight.

Beth: Am I going to like it?

Winnie: Please tell me the jerks are getting what is coming to them.

Sarah: Come on guys. Everything is just calming down. Do we really want to start something up?

Beth: YES

Winnie: YES

Jesse: Listen, I worked hard on this, and it is happening. It took me five different times of sneaking in to make it happen. T minus four hours. Prepare for Jessegeddon to commence.

Remington: Thanks for the heads up. Should I invite Baron and Regina over with the kids?

Jesse: No one will get hurt. They might wish they were dead.

Trying to control her sisters was like trying to herd cats. Thank goodness Jesse had warned her and she could avoid whatever she had planned. She agreed the guys definitely deserved it. She wasn't sure who had put frosting coloring in

Beth's lotion, but it had taken a week for the green tinge to wear off. Winnie had gotten doused when she'd opened the door to the shop right before she was set to leave for a job.

Most of their pranks had been annoying but then she hadn't been the target recently. She'd wait to see what Jesse had done and then take appropriate action if needed.

As she and War had grown closer, she'd had the crazy dream of maybe her sisters would all marry men from the MC. She thought she had them all picked out, but a couple of her sisters seemed furious at the men. It was probably a pipe dream, but she could hope. Right now, she needed to make sure everything was perfect for the reopening of the gym.

"I'm back," Winnie walked in, tears pooling in her eyes.

Remington slid an arm around her shoulders. "I told you we'd rebuild."

Winnie nodded. "I knew we eventually would but each week we weren't open, I worried. Now, it's bigger, better but still with the safety features. Is biker prez coming tonight?"

"I know he's hoping he will."

Winnie rolled her eyes. "Childish."

"Maybe so but it got you to smile. Let's finish up and get ready for people."

War munched on another chocolate chip cookie. Beth had made them, and he was addicted. He wondered if anyone would notice if he filled a sack and hid it on his bike. The only thing missing was a cold glass of milk. His choices were tea, lemonade and water. He'd make do but he knew what he'd be asking Beth to make him for Christmas—a gallon bag of cookies. Since Christmas was still a couple months away, maybe he should see if he could bribe her with something. He had to go shopping for Remi's ring. If he worked it right, maybe she'd make him more.

His woman was greeting people and helping people sign up for classes. The only concession Remi had made to the occasion was adding some silver bracelets and a necklace over a sparkling top. Despite the additions, her jeans and boots screamed badass.

He wanted to lock Remi down and have his ring on her finger, but his woman had dreams. Dreams he was determined to fulfill, including his badass woman having the perfect proposal, a wedding with all her sisters and a party to end all parties. Her words. He wouldn't have thought she'd want that, but his Remi was multi-faceted. He looked forward to uncovering new things as they grew old.

Watching her in her thigh-hugging jeans, he wanted to find a supply closet, bathroom, or something to assuage his need but then he'd gotten used to it. One glance at her and he wanted her on any surface.

He was also looking forward to waking up beside her and enjoying a leisurely morning. She'd mentioned riding his bike to the open market tomorrow morning. He'd threatened his officers to leave him alone. Unless they were under attack, he should be able to have one weekend with Remington. She'd already volunteered them for babysitting next week. She'd set Roam up and was forcing him to go out with someone. Roam had already said he wasn't interested in anything long-term, but his woman had a one-track mind.

She wanted everyone as happy as she was.

Chapter Thirty-Two

War patted Remi's hands wrapped around his waist. He'd been ecstatic when Remi said she wanted to ride with him for the Toy Run. They were outside their last destination—Dodge City. Whiskey's family had stepped up and was feeding all the riders and helping with the distribution of the toys. One of the security team members was driving a box truck full of toys plus they all had a couple on their motorcycles.

They were fifteen minutes from the bar and his time was up. He'd given himself until Thanksgiving to open up to Remi about the incident but as the weeks passed, he kept putting it off. He'd imagined with the Toy Run the Saturday before Thanksgiving it would be the perfect time. Plus he wouldn't have to see the condemnation in her eyes.

Bear had called him a dumbass multiple times with Cannon, Scoop and Flick chiming in their agreement. Whether he was a dumbass or not, he had big plans for Christmas with Remington and he needed a clean slate to do that.

Countless times on the ride he'd started to share then paused. Remi loved him and he hoped and prayed this didn't change her opinion of him.

"I wanted to share something with you, but I don't want you to say anything until the end." He paused, waiting for her agreement. Maybe not seeing her face was a bad idea. Her eyes were so expressive, and he couldn't tell what she was thinking. Her arms squeezed a little, then one hand reached his thigh and patted.

"Okay."

He swallowed, hoping he could get through this without throwing up. Wouldn't that be a sight on the Toy Run! The president pulling over to blow chunks on the side of the road.

"You asked about my greatest regret on our first date. I gave you an easy answer. My greatest regret is the day my trainee died. I should have bounced her from the program, but Bear had been her training officer. He'd been hurt. I was worried about him and didn't want to second guess his opinion. I didn't know he'd come to the same conclusion. She had family high up in the local government but that isn't an excuse. We went to a call, and she did her *I know better* routine and didn't follow orders. She was shot and bled out before the ambulance could get there. I didn't realize how much her attitude changed how I looked at females in the department and later, in the security company. I want you to know I see you, my warrior woman, and not her incompetence. You and your sisters have shown me I can't let a horrible incident change my view of all women."

He'd thrown it all out there. It was up to Remington now.

Her arms hugged him as she whispered, "I love you, War. I appreciate you opening up, but I already knew about the incident. You hold no culpability in her death. She'd been given multiple opportunities. She should never had been assigned a new training officer after Bear's shooting. Your chief should have put her on leave and at least investigated."

"How do you know all that?"

He was thrilled Remington didn't think less of him. He was also positive Bear wouldn't have broken any confidence.

"War, I deal in security, meaning I have to know any things in a person's background before I assign them to a detail. Sarah ran deep backgrounds on each of you and when she does a deep dive, nothing is left out. I never brought it up because you didn't mention it."

He chuckled. Of course they did deep dives into their security personnel. He'd worried for nothing but hearing Remington's view on the incident released the last bit of guilt he had. In all the times he'd gone over the incident, he'd never considered the chief shouldn't have reassigned her.

"If we weren't on this bike in the middle of all our friends, I'd pull over and show you how much you mean to me."

Remington's hands slid down his stomach, one sliding underneath his shirt, lightly scratching his belly.

"Let's save that thought."

He turned down the street and followed Winnie's hand signals directing them to the bike parking in the street. He shut down and waited for Remi to get off the bike. Whiskey was walking toward him with a microphone and a piece of paper. He glanced at the numbers on the paper, cocking his eyebrow at Whiskey.

"These are correct?"

"Yes. We scrambled to get another bin for the toys and Winnie and Sarah confirmed the cash numbers."

War jumped up on the podium as the last of the bikes stopped and shut down.

"Welcome, Bluff Creek Brotherhood MC and friends." He paused, waiting for the yelling and whistling to die down. "I want to thank the Nelson family for volunteering their bar as our last stop and coordinating food, drink and drop off for us. When I came back to the MC, I was ready for change. Instead of the worst of humanity getting away with things, I wanted to make a difference. I thought I'd need to change and implement new things but what I found was the foundation was already built. Today, each of you have helped make someone's Christmas a little better. The current numbers, which could change as we are accepting donations through today, are: one hundred and fifty thousand toys, cash donations of sixty-five thousand, three hundred dollars, and fifteen thousand cans of food. I admit I'm stunned. I don't know if this is the most we've ever done or not."

"It's more than double our highest year!" Baron yelled.

"Thanks, Dad. Some of you may not know my background. When I was three, my mom took a chance because, through no fault of her own, we were days away from being homeless. Her decision led us to the place where my brother and I would find a father and numerous men who became uncles. They showed us how real men lived. I still remember that first Christmas with them when they made all our dreams come true and showed us their generous spirits. That's the feeling we will be giving to someone. Your generosity will brighten someone's life who otherwise might not have anything. Now, let's eat!"

Remington pulled a tissue out and wiped her eyes, then blew her nose. Her man with his tattoos, cut and angular jaw may be tough but inside where it mattered, he cared. She stood back, watching him receive congratulations and slaps on the back from the huge amount of bikers today.

Today was one of those feel-good days where everything was right with the world. She and War both saw a lot of the worst of humanity, so she vowed to always cherish these perfect days. The days when they were all together and hopefully, there weren't any pranks. She along with War were getting a little tired of them but she had to admit, her sister's had been devious.

The men were still complaining about the last one. Jesse had done something to the clubhouse and from eleven o'clock at night until seven in the morning, no one could leave the clubhouse. Normally, it wouldn't be a problem because they'd just sleep, watch TV, etc. She wasn't sure how they'd done it, but no one had been able to access any adult sites in the clubhouse. They'd also had every TV and phone play *Hannah Montana* shows and music. When she mentioned she would just sleep, Winnie giggled and said even if they went to sleep alarms went off all night every half hour playing "Who Said" to remind them women could be anything. She only hoped her sisters were ready for what the MC did to get back and that she was far, far away. She wasn't going to worry about that. She was going to grab her man and go enjoy some barbecue in the bar.

Tomorrow would be soon enough to worry about anything else but even with worries, her heart was lighter knowing War would be by her side. She was giving him until New Year's Eve, though, and if he hadn't moved their relationship along with a proposal or property cut, she'd be taking matters into her hands. A tattoo across his head of *TAKEN* might be too extreme but she'd like something to keep the women who came to party with the club away.

Her man left the group congratulating him, striding toward her, his smile ear to ear with happiness. Yes, today was a fantastic day. She'd need to figure out some way for alone time with her man to celebrate.

"What say you and I grab some food then see if we can find a private place for me to show you some appreciation?"

"It sounds like you're the perfect man for me. Let's go!"

Chapter Thirty- Three

Remington picked up another piece of wrapping paper and stuffed it in the trash sack. Her need for everything in its place wouldn't allow her to wait until all the presents were opened before cleaning up. Even the mess didn't dim her happiness today.

She loved everything about Christmas, but this Christmas with War was a dream come true. Her family was whole and healthy, and she'd found the man who she couldn't live without. Although for some reason, he still enjoyed playing pranks on her occasionally. The confetti blowing out of her car last week was a case in point. She'd tried to act irritated but let's face it, one of their love languages was playing pranks. She and her sisters were meeting next week to plan a couple for January and February.

The months were so cold sometimes, they had to find some fun. Regina was in her element, making sure everyone felt welcome. Some people might find the level of noise annoying but to Remington, it meant everyone could be themselves.

War made his way through the kids on the floor, grabbing a couple of pieces of wrapping paper to put in her trash bag. His eyes ran down her then looked her in the eye as he tossed her trash bag to Roam. Tugging her toward the middle of the room, he grinned, looking up toward the mistletoe above their heads.

He didn't waste any time claiming her lips and only stopped when the yelling and clapping was continuous. Pulling his lips away, he held her hand as he knelt in front of her.

"Remington Rachel Franks, we've had a long road to get here. Probably because I'm too hard-headed to see the beauty that was always in front of me." He paused for the laughter to quiet. "It may have taken until I was forty-four years old, but I know what I want now. I've been given a glimpse of how wonderful life can be with you by my side. I love your strength, your decisiveness, and I've even fallen in love with your need for a neat house. Each day, I wake up excited to spend it with you, my love. There's nothing I'd change about you because you're perfect for me. I want to spend the rest of my life showing how much you mean to me. Whether we live in your current house or build a brand new one, I don't care because the place doesn't matter—you do. My warrior woman, will you marry me?"

She swallowed, trying to find enough moisture to answer. "I always wondered why I couldn't find anyone over the years but then you came home. I realized I'd found my hero years ago but had to wait for us to find our way back to each other. I can't think of anything I want more than to be yours. Yes, I'm yours always."

He slid the ring on her finger and had her in his arms in seconds. The place she'd always dreamed of being was hers now and forever. He was right, their road had been bumpy, but she wouldn't change a thing. They weren't starry-eyed kids who didn't know what they wanted. They'd grow old together while raising a family. She couldn't wait to tell him they'd already begun. Maybe she'd save that nugget to share with him when they were alone. She loved their huge family but for a little while, she wanted to keep it to just them. She and her biker president who'd given her the world. She didn't need a prince to rescue her. She had her man who recognized they could stand together against anything.

He turned and held his hand out. She might be a badass woman, but she'd longed for a property cut. She'd hoped War would continue the tradition. He turned back, holding her cut.

"I know there'll only be certain times you can wear this because of your job but when you can, I want everyone to know you're mine. Will you ride with me until we leave this earth?"

She nodded, helping him slip it on her shoulders. When their family started yelling and clapping, he held up his hand.

"When Sarah, Mom and your sisters were sewing the patch on yours, I realized besides having Roam tattoo you over my heart, I wanted something visible on my cut."

She looked and spotted the new patch she'd missed. *Property of Remington* curved over two berettas mimicking her tattoo. Underneath was written, *trespassers will be shot on sight.* She giggled, leaning over and taking his lips. He couldn't have made her any happier today. Granted, it wasn't a tattoo on his forehead but the fact he was the first man in the MC with an ol' lady to allow a patch designating him as her property was perfect.

War kept Remington close to his side as his family congratulated them. Until he came back, he hadn't realized how much he was missing. Whether by blood or by choice, they were one big family ready to defend each other.

He'd known he needed to figure out how to ask his woman to marry him. After getting everyone's opinions, he'd decided to go with his gut. Christmas at Bluff Creek Brotherhood had changed his life forty years ago. It had seemed the perfect time to make the next step. A step where the woman he couldn't live without became his wife officially.

They were practically living together anyway. He and Remington had talked late one night about whether they would continue using both places. He'd moved into one of the one-bedroom houses on the property. Depending on what was on their calendar, they took turns staying at either the house at BCB or at her house on the bail bonds compound. Since they'd bought Clancey's land, Beth's design included a new place for houses a little more protected. He hoped Remington wanted to build something new that was just theirs. They'd been adding tunnels for a couple different buildings, and he'd love to incorporate that into their housing.

Bear pulled Remington out of his arms and into Bear's for a hug, pulling his thoughts from houses to beating up his best friend for kissing Remington's cheek.

"Congratulations, Remi. You let me know if he gets out of line."

Before Remi could answer, War tugged Remington back closer again and growled, "Mine," at his friend.

Bear chuckled, turning back to take money from Rascal, Baron and Locks.

"Seriously, you three?"

Before he had a chance to tear into them, their prospect walked into the room.

"Prez, there's a sheriff's car and another car requesting entrance to the clubhouse. They said they need to speak to a Benton Carter."

War looked toward his best friend, Bear. Why would the sheriff's department need Bear?

"Let them in. Take the kids to a back bedroom. Any idea what this is about?"

Bear shook his head, waiting for them to walk in. The deputy held the door as a woman carrying a baby carrier and holding the hand of small child walked in, followed by another older child.

"Benton Carter?" the woman questioned. The oldest child saw Bear and ran toward him, throwing her arms around him.

"Officer Bear, Mommy's gone to Heaven." Her words choked off as she started sobbing.

Bear lifted her up, letting her wrap her arms around him. He patted her back, squeezing his eyes shut for a minute then opening them and answering the woman.

"Yes, I'm Benton."

"I'm with social services. Cassidy Glickson listed you as the father on all three birth certificates and named you as who the children go to in case of her death. An incident happened and she passed away."

"Go to him, War," Remington whispered.

He strode over to Bear. He recognized the name of a prostitute they'd arrested a couple times. About a month before they'd come back home, Bear had said he couldn't handle those kids doing without. He said they reminded him of his childhood before Rascal brought him home. Now that he thought about it, after Bear mentioned that they'd never seen her out again.

"Bear, what do you need?"

Bear's eyes looked scared but determined.

"I guess I need help figuring out where we're going to stay. What do you need so they stay with me?" Bear questioned, patting the young girl's back as she continued to cry.

War wiped the tears from his eyes, not caring who saw them. His warrior woman had given him the greatest gift—a beautiful baby girl with her eyes. He knew Remi was strong but watching her go through eight hours of labor without a scream was amazing.

"She looks just like you did, Remi," Locks whispered, leaning over to kiss Remington's forehead. "I wish your mama could see you, War, and this beautiful baby girl. She was always positive you two would get together in your own time."

His dad and mom crowded a little closer, his mom patting his arm while Baron wrapped his arm around both of them.

"She'll be a heartbreaker," Baron commented.

"She'll be a badass like her mother and father," Regina retorted.

Knowing their child, she'd probably be both. He and Remi were both strong-willed and hardheaded.

"Okay, the grandparents have had their turn. Scoot away so we can all see our niece."

A chorus of yeahs had all the sisters agreeing with Winnie. When Remi had informed him that she wanted a family birth with everyone in the family suite to have the baby, he'd been skeptical, but it was perfect.

A couple of times when he didn't know how he was going to allow Remi to continue hurting, his dad and Locks had patted his shoulder and given him words to get through it. When Remi had been getting tired and looked at him and whispered she wasn't sure how much longer she could do it, her sisters had rallied around with encouraging words and reminded Remi how strong she was.

His baby girl had a huge family to help her grow up but for right now, he wanted to enjoy her being small enough to fit in his arms. He couldn't wait until they were home and could cuddle together. Not that they'd be alone even there. He could imagine he might need to put some type of lock on his doors if he wanted to get a little time alone with his girls. Considering their houses were all together, it wasn't unusual for all of them to gravitate to one of the houses. With the addition of their little one, it would most likely be theirs.

"What's her name?"

War smiled. They had chosen multiple names since they didn't want to find out what they were having before the birth. They'd had a whiteboard of their favorites, keeping it hidden in their closet so the family couldn't give their opinions. He and Remington had enough problems picking just between the two of them.

"Amelia Kathryn Shields. Amelia because of the boundaries Amelia Earhart broke and Kathryn for Mom. We want her to know that there are no limits to what she can do." Remi's words had her sister's smiling.

"I'll teach her how to take care of her car."

"She and I can be gym buddies."

"I imagine after a little time, she'll be running circles around me on the computer."

"Aunty Beth will be teaching her about surveillance and where to buy the best clothes."

Her sisters' comments flew fast and furious. He had no doubts that Amelia would be well loved. Maybe now he could convince Remington the compound needed the barbed wire added to keep their little warrior safe.

The End

Thank you for reading War. If you loved he and Remi's story, your rating or honest review will help future readers decide if they want to take a chance on a new-to-them author. I can't thank you enough for taking a chance on this new series. There are a lot more stories coming in the Bluff Creek Brotherhood Mc.

Bear is the next in series. I've included a little excerpt here.

Bear laid still, trying not to disturb who was next to him. He flipped through his memories of last night working to understand how they'd ended up like this. Not that he hadn't wanted her forever.

The first time he recognized her as the woman she'd become, he'd been home on leave from the Army. He's been thirty-three and she'd been twenty-three. The song he heard when he noticed her *Drops of Jupiter* still made him think of that first glimpse of her whenever he heard it. She'd had on tight jeans and a black tank top with the bail bonds logo on it in neon green highlighting her breasts. Exactly where he shouldn't be looking once, he'd realized she was Locks middle daughter and the younger sister of his only female friend. She'd been grinning and laughing at something one of her sisters had said. He'd craved walking over into her presence just to have a little of her sunshine.

The second time he'd denied himself, he'd been forty and she'd been thirty. He'd left the army, joined the police force, and had made detective. Her family had been building a gym and wanted his expertise in planning for the unexpected. He was good at that- thinking of the worst-case scenario. It's how his brain worked. If he could think through all the worst things that could happen, he could plan for them. It helped him feel like he had a semblance of control over his life. He'd helped on the gym plans all the while trying to not fall for her. Between her bringing him healthy food because she deemed, he needed to eat better and her trying to get him to work out with her, he'd lost the battle. Lifting weights beside her, it was all he could do to keep his dick from having a life of its own. She wasn't like the women he usually picked up for a couple of nights. She was toned with small breasts, almost small enough to not need a bra but it didn't stop him from wanting her. She was off limits- friend's little sister and daughter of an original in the MC. Plus ten fucking years between them was a lot. He'd experienced things in the Army that had changed him and later as a police officer, he'd seen the worst of humanity. It might be ten years but he felt ancient next to her with her grin he craved to see.

The third time he'd denied himself was when he and his friends had moved home for good to the MC, a little over three and a half months ago. Everything about her called to him but he was grumpy on his good days and downright snarly and unapproachable on his bad days- which happened a lot. She was a breath of fresh air on a hot humid day. She was the sun when he could only see darkness, but he couldn't take the chance he would ruin her.

Obviously, he was an asshole though because her head was lying on his shoulder, her hair tickling his neck which is what had woken him. Her toned thigh was over his.

They'd been coming back from a three-day security gig. He'd kept it professional the whole time though it had worn on him. He found himself gravitating close to her because she was one of the few women he enjoyed being around. He kept most at a distance.

They'd been driving back from Topeka when the tornado warning had come through. If they'd continued home, they'd drive right into the warning area. He wasn't willing to risk them both when it was dark, and they couldn't even see if something was coming. They'd found one room available with a queen-size bed. He'd decided he'd sleep on the floor because he wasn't sure he could keep his hands to himself. What an understatement. Holding her in his arms had started as a craving but built to a tsunami of need. It was all he could do to stop himself from reaching over in the SUV to feel her touch.

When the thunderstorm had come through, he'd heard her whimper. She was so fucking strong, but thunderstorms and the threat of tornadoes freaked her out. He knew there was a reason he shouldn't crawl into bed with her but with her staring at him over the edge of the bed, his blood had all gone south, and he wasn't thinking clearly.

Winnie had asked him to come up on the bed. From there, he hadn't been able to resist. Her soft lips against his neck, her hand trailing down his torso as he held the most precious thing in the world against him.

He could maybe forgive himself if it had been a one-off but after he'd had her once, he reached for her two more times. He'd had to taste her. Feeling her thighs shake while he slaked his thirst was seared into his brain. Each time Winnie had came, she'd whimpered his given name Benton- not his road name. If he thought he wouldn't ruin her, he'd take her home and never let her go.

It had been the best night of his life, but he couldn't let it go on. She deserved sunshine, roses, and a family. His life wasn't for her...

Bear released Oct. 26, 2023. The best way to stay in touch is to be a part of my newsletter. If you aren't on my list yet, grab my free prequel here: https://dl.bookfunnel.com/fbvhukvk7f You'll get a free book. I share excerpts as I'm writing and you'll be the first to know when Bear is up for preorder.

Once again, thank you so much for reading War.